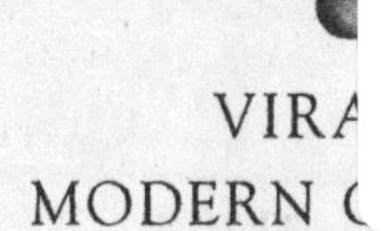

VIRA
MODERN C
594

Angela Thirkell

Angela Thirkell (1890–1961) was the eldest daughter of John William Mackail, a Scottish classical scholar and civil servant, and Margaret Burne-Jones. Her relatives included the pre-Raphaelite artist Edward Burne-Jones, Rudyard Kipling and Stanley Baldwin, and her godfather was J. M. Barrie. She was educated in London and Paris, and began publishing articles and stories in the 1920s. In 1931 she brought out her first book, a memoir entitled *Three Houses*, and in 1933 her comic novel *High Rising* – set in the fictional county of Barsetshire, borrowed from Trollope – met with great success. She went on to write nearly thirty Barsetshire novels, as well as several further works of fiction and non-fiction. She was twice married, and had four children.

By Angela Thirkell

Barsetshire novels

High Rising
Wild Strawberries
The Demon in the House
August Folly
Summer Half
Pomfret Towers
The Brandons
Before Lunch
Cheerfulness Breaks In
Northbridge Rectory
Marling Hall
Growing Up
The Headmistress
Miss Bunting
Peace Breaks Out
Private Enterprise
Love Among the Ruins
The Old Bank House
County Chronicle
The Duke's Daughter
Happy Returns
Jutland Cottage
What Did it Mean?
Enter Sir Robert
Never Too Late
A Double Affair
Close Quarters
Love at All Ages
Three Score and Ten

Non-fiction

Three Houses

Collected stories

Christmas at High Rising

CHRISTMAS AT HIGH RISING

Angela Thirkell

virago

VIRAGO

This collection first published in 2013 by Virago Press
Reprinted 2013

Copyright © the Estate of Angela Thirkell 1928, 1934,
1935, 1936, 1937, 1940, 1942
Copyright in the collection © the Estate of Angela Thirkell 2013

The moral right of the author has been asserted.

All characters and events in this publication, other than those clearly in the public domain, are fictitious and any resemblance to real persons, living or dead, is purely coincidental.

All rights reserved.
No part of this publication may be reproduced, stored in a retrieval system, or transmitted in any form or by any means, without the prior permission in writing of the publisher, nor be otherwise circulated in any form of binding or cover other than that in which it is published and without a similar condition including this condition being imposed on the subsequent purchaser.

A CIP catalogue record for this book
is available from the British Library.

ISBN 978-0-349-00430-3

Typeset in Goudy by M Rules
Printed and bound in Great Britain by
Clays Ltd, St Ives plc

Papers used by Virago are from well-managed forests
and other responsible sources.

MIX
Paper from
responsible sources
FSC® C104740

Virago Press
An imprint of
Little, Brown Book Group
100 Victoria Embankment
London EC4Y 0DY

An Hachette UK Company
www.hachette.co.uk

www.virago.co.uk

Contents

Pantomime

George Knox, the celebrated biographer, who was incapable of doing things by halves, and indeed capable only of overdoing them, suddenly felt that as a grandfather he ought to take a large family party to the theatre. In vain did his wife point out to him that his granddaughter, being barely six months old, would certainly not be allowed to come and could not appreciate it if she did, and that the rest of his family, which consisted of his married daughter Sibyl Coates and her husband Adrian, would far rather stay in warmth and comfort in his house at Low Rising where they were staying on a visit. George Knox, who had already begun to dramatise himself as Famous Author Loves to Gather Little Ones Round Him, was so dejected by her words that she had to give in, only stipulating that he should consult their neighbour, Mrs Morland, before doing anything rash.

'Because, as far as I can see, George,' she said, 'Tony is

the only child we can get hold of, unless you wanted to take the Vicarage girls. You had better go over to High Rising and talk to Laura about it.'

So George Knox dressed himself in a large hat and muffler as Famous Author Takes Country Walk, and went over to High Rising. Here he found Mrs Morland at tea.

'Sit down, George, and have some tea,' said Laura, 'because you won't have any peace in a few moments. Tony and Rose and Dora Gould insist on acting charades to me, which is terribly dull. Luckily, they take about ten times as long to get their scenes ready as they do to act them, so you can talk between whiles.'

George Knox gratefully accepted a cup of tea and began to develop his plan for a family pantomime party, but before Laura had even begun to have the faintest idea of what he was talking about, the door burst open, and Rose was pushed in by unseen powers whose voices could be heard whispering encouragement to her from the hall. Rose advanced diffidently to Mrs Morland and twisted herself about in embarrassment.

'Well, what is it, Rose?' said Laura.

'Please, Mrs Morland,' said Rose in a painful whisper, 'Tony says can we have Mr Knox's hat for our next scene?'

'Certainly not,' said Laura.

The unseen powers suddenly became silent.

'You have all got hats of your own,' said Laura. 'Use one of them.'

'Of course,' said one of the unseen powers in a voice remarkably like Tony's, 'if we can't have the hat it's all absolutely no good. People don't seem to understand that one must have proper hats to do acting properly.'

'But, my dear Laura,' said George Knox, 'why this curmudgeonly attitude towards property which, after all, is not yours and for which, therefore, you need feel no responsibility? If at this festive season a hat more or less, be it mine, be it whose you will – or would it perhaps be more correct, if less euphonious, to say whose you will's, but a truce to these idle questions – if, I say, a hat can give pleasure to man, bird, or beast, why should this pleasure be denied?'

'Well, George,' said Laura, 'you can't exactly call Tony and the girls men or birds or beasts, but if you don't mind them having your hat, that's your look out. All right, Rose, then you can have the hat.'

Rose retired in speechless confusion.

'This will be the whole word,' said Laura to George Knox. 'They have done three syllables and there is no doubt that they were Core and Lie and Flower, so the whole word will be "cauliflower", but don't guess at once, because they will be so disappointed. I couldn't help guessing the other syllables because Tony won't let the girls say them and when he says them himself he says them so loud that one simply can't help knowing, however hard one tries not to.'

The final scene of the charade exceeded Laura's worst expectations. Rose and Dora were supposed to keep a vegetable shop and Tony to be a regular customer, though attired as he was in Rose's coat with a little fur collar and George Knox's hat, which was only prevented by his bat-like ears from extinguishing him entirely, he had a sinister appearance which would have made any nervous shopkeeper suspect him at once. After a long pointless conversation conducted almost entirely by Tony, who, to his mother's horror, pretended to be drunk in a very lifelike way, he took off his hat, made a sweeping bow to the audience, and left the room.

'Tony, Tony,' shrieked the two little girls, 'the word!'

Tony returned, full of calm confidence, and approaching the temporary counter said, 'I happen to have forgotten another vegetable that I wanted.'

'I know what you want,' said Dora, 'a cau—'

'You can't know what I want, because I haven't said it,' interrupted Tony quickly. 'And I don't suppose your shop has it, so it isn't much use my asking for it. It would have been a CAULIFLOWER. That's the end. Do you know what the word is?'

'Is it "potato"?' asked the weak-minded Laura.

'Oh, Mother!'

'Or "asparagus"?'

'Mother! "Asparagus" has four syllables.'

'I know it, my boy, I know it,' said George Knox with eager complacency. 'In fact, none but a moron, and such I flatter myself I am not, though I make no pretension to intellect, could have been in doubt as to the word. It was – and I shall make no bones – a phrase, Laura, as to whose provenance I am in doubt – no circumlocutions, about telling you the conclusion at which I have arrived, a conclusion which—'

'It was a jolly good charade, sir, wasn't it?' said Tony with honest pride. 'I invented it all. Rose and Dora haven't much idea of acting, but I acted in the school play, so I know all about acting, and I trained them. They haven't much idea of talking yet, but I can do the talking. I have a kind of gift for talking.'

'To tell me that fact,' said George Knox, 'is a work of supererogation, my boy. But as I was saying, the word which it is, I gather, my part in this entertainment to guess, that word is—'

'George!' interrupted Laura reproachfully.

At the same moment George Knox's hat came right down over Tony's face, causing him to stumble over the counter and all the vegetables to fall on the floor. Tony got up and removed himself from the hat.

'The word was "cauliflower",' he said, picking up the scattered potatoes and onions and putting them into George Knox's hat. 'I should have thought you would have guessed that, sir. I made it easy on purpose for you, because you aren't very practised. I would have guessed it at once.'

'But I did guess it,' cried George Knox, much annoyed. 'But for you and your mother, who make it impossible for me, a man of taciturn humour, ever ready to put himself in the background, to get a word in edgeways, I should long ago have told you the word. And take those onions out of my hat at once,' he added in fury.

'Yes, take them out at once, Tony,' said Laura. 'Mr Knox is going to take us all to the pantomime on Saturday.'

'Oh, Mother! That's the day the hounds meet near Southbridge and Dr Ford has promised to take me. Need I?'

'It can't be helped. Mr Knox has determined to take us all to the pantomime,' said Laura rather ungratefully, 'and there it is.'

'I dare say Rose and Dora will enjoy it,' said Tony. 'It's rather a treat for kids, of course. Can I wear my trouser suit, mother? And shall I have my school tie or the one I bought for myself for one and sixpence halfpenny? It's a jolly good tie, sir,' he said, turning to George Knox. 'If you want to know a good shop for ties, come to me, sir.'

Laura now had to apply herself to pacifying George Knox, suppressing Tony, and calming Rose and Dora. Luckily, the Vicarage cook arrived to fetch the girls, and as she was on extremely bad terms with Stoker the maid, she had her young charges out of the house in no time.

'Now, George,' said Laura, 'this is an awful treat that you want to give us, but I suppose we shall have to give in. I know Anne and Adrian and Sibyl don't want to come. Couldn't I and the three children be a sacrifice for the rest? After all, you can't take five grown-ups and three children even in your luxurious Rolls Royce, and I am certainly not going to drive my car up to London and back on Saturday, besides all the parking difficulties. And you are not going to hire another car, which is what I see in your eye, so we will do as I say. And after all you will look much more like a grandfather if you have three children with you than if you have a lot of grown-ups. I wouldn't come myself, because I hate pantomimes, but I feel you need help with the children.'

George Knox submitted and seats were procured. On the evening of Friday, Mrs Gould rang up Low Rising to say that Rose had not slept all night, had been violently over-excited all day, and was now in bed with a temperature and the beginning of one of her bad colds. Anne Knox then implored her stepson-in-law, Adrian Coates, to take Rose's place, so that George Knox might not be disappointed of a guest.

'Sibyl and I would so hate to go,' said Anne, 'that words could not express it. So will you be a sacrifice, Adrian?'

Accordingly, at eleven o'clock on Saturday the Rolls

Royce collected George Knox (carrying a plaid and walking stick in his self-appointed role as grandfather), Adrian, Dora, Laura and Tony from their separate abodes and took them all to London, where Adrian proposed to give them lunch at his club. As they entered the club, Tony, who had been made by common consent to sit beside the chauffeur, to whom he had given a good deal of valuable if erroneous information about racing motors and their engines, assumed the devil-may-care attitude of a man of the world and, having given his coat and school cap to the attendant, walked off nonchalantly in the wrong direction, followed by Dora.

'Hi, Tony, come back,' Adrian called after him, 'that's for members only.'

Tony gave Adrian a glance of passionless scorn and followed him to the dining-room. Here, the conversation not unnaturally turned on the pantomime which they were to see.

'What is it, by the way, George?' asked Laura, in whom want of curiosity almost amounted to a vice.

'*Aladdin*,' said Tony. 'Mother, didn't you know it was *Aladdin*? Mother, Dora hadn't ever read it, so I was sorry for her being so uneducated and I told her the story.'

He broke open a large roll, put four pats of butter into it, shut it up again, and began to devour it.

'You won't have any appetite left if you eat all that bread to begin with,' said Adrian.

'But, sir, I'm hungry.'

'Is there any reason, Adrian, why my child should not eat if he is hungry?' said Laura majestically.

Adrian was so quelled by this remark that he did not like to protest when Tony, having put about an ounce of pepper into his soup, sneezed until his friends began to despair of his recovery, nor when he took his chicken's wishbone in his fingers and gnawed it as clean as Bishop Hatto. But when, to impress Dora, he put a whole mince-pie into his mouth at once, his mother, who had been talking earnestly to George Knox, suddenly became aware of him.

'No, Tony. Not all in your mouth at once,' said she in a voice which immediately commanded the attention of all the neighbouring tables. But it was too late, and Tony was obliged to do a great deal of violent masticating before he could get enough mouth-room to exculpate himself.

'But, Mother, Dora is rather sad because Rose can't come, aren't you, Dora? So I was amusing her. I thought you liked me to be kind to people, Mother. Can I have another mince-pie, because I'm hungry?'

When Laura looked round the second mince-pie had vanished with such celerity that she expected to see her son burst before her eyes, but as he appeared to be quite well, and Dora was giggling with admiration, she only told Tony to wipe some of the pastry crumbs off his mouth, a request which he took in very bad part, flapping his face with his table napkin as one who was being taken upon and overdriven by Egyptian taskmasters. Just then, George Knox discovered it was high time to be off, so the children were hustled into their coats and the party got into the car. Tony asked to be allowed to drive inside.

'I thought you liked driving with the chauffeur,' said Laura.

'Well, Mother, that's all very well in the country, but in London it's rather different. One of the chaps who was up for the hols might see me.'

Laura was prepared to be unsympathetic, but Adrian, who remembered how tremendously the opinion of one's school friends mattered at that age, kindly squashed him into the car.

'If there had been more of us, I should have taken the front row of the dress circle,' said George Knox sadly, 'but as things are, I have got a box.'

At this news Tony and Dora gasped. Neither of them had ever been in a box before and this represented the most romantic of their dreams. Tony was the first to recover his poise.

'Of course, I always sit in the Royal Box in my Morland theatre,' he said carelessly, 'but I just happen not to have been in one in London. You can't have been in one in Dorland,' he added hastily to Dora, 'because your

Dorland theatre hasn't got any boxes, only stalls and dress circle.'

But when the full glory of the best box with a private sitting-room behind it burst upon his view, Tony was for once entirely silenced. In a holy rapture he wandered from one to the other, drinking in their glories, their red satin curtains, their gilded chairs with red plush seats. Finally, with a sigh of satisfaction, he established himself in an armchair, assuming the world-weary expression of one who is satiated with the gayer side of life. Laura and Adrian sat behind, putting George Knox, as professional grandfather and founder of the feast, in front with the two children. George enjoyed every moment with loud and violent appreciation. Laura was bored nearly to distraction, but found pleasure in watching her son's profile, silhouetted against the dazzling lights of the stage, immobile except for an occasional twitch. It was evident that he considered any outward manifestation of pleasure as beneath his dignity. Even tea and cakes in the private sitting-room could not break down his stoical attitude, and he returned to his seat without having committed himself by a single word.

'Well, my boy,' said George Knox as the curtain fell for the second interval. 'And how do you like it?'

'It's fairly decent, sir,' said Tony kindly. 'I should think the princess is quite about twenty-five, but she looks quite young. I don't think much of the band, do you, sir? It's—'

Here he broke off and turned to his mother. His face was alight with enthusiasm and his voice had lost all its world-weariness as he pulled his mother by her dress, exclaiming in a loud voice, 'Oh, Mother, *who* do you think I've seen?'

'The Prince of Wales?' said Laura, looking wildly round.

'Mother! I mean really important. Look, Mother, over there in the dress circle. It's old Donk. Mother, do you think he can see me? What will he think when he sees me in a box, Mother? Can I go and talk to him? Mother, he hasn't seen me yet. I'll hypnotise him to make him see me.'

'You can't,' said Dora. 'Hypnotism's all rubbish. Daddy said so.'

'I bet you I can,' said Tony, and hanging over the edge of the box in a way which caused his mother's heart to palpitate with anxiety, he made various cabalistic signs, which if they did not succeed in hypnotising Master Wesendonck to look, at least attracted the attention of the greater part of the audience.

'Tony! Don't lean over like that,' said his agonised mother. 'You'll fall into the orchestra and be killed.'

But before this misfortune could occur, Master Wesendonck's eye had been caught. Tony gave a gasp of relief and sank back into his chair, from which he waved a languid hand at his friend, followed by various grimaces which evidently alluded to school jokes and were taken in excellent part by his fellow-pupil. All too soon the curtain rose again for the last act, but Tony's spirits were now completely restored. Delicious high-pitched laughter broke uncontrollably from him at intervals. When the Widow Twankey became entangled in the clothes-horse and the mangle, he rocked backwards and forwards in an ecstasy of joy, kicking the front of the box with his shoes and making the legs of his chair bump on the ground with the vehemence of his pleasure. Wrapt in a romantic trance, drunk with the Widow and overjoyed by the presence of his friend among the audience, he was impervious to the tweaks and hushes from his elders. By the time the performance ended, all three grown-ups were cross and exhausted, but Tony rose radiant from his seat.

'Jolly good performance,' he said kindly to his host. 'Mother, did you hear me laughing at the funny parts? I have a good kind of laugh and I expect the actors liked it. I wonder if Donk heard me, Mother. Mr Knox, can we wait at the door and see if we can see Donk?'

Laura gave no encouragement to this plan, but by the greatest good luck as they stood waiting for George Knox's car, Master Wesendonck, supported by a mother and sisters, hove in sight.

'Hullo, Donk,' said Tony in a loud voice. 'Pretty rotten show, wasn't it, but I laughed at some of the bits. Did you hear me laughing? I was in a box.'

Master Wesendonck nodded silently and passed on.

'Good old Donk,' said Tony contentedly. 'He enjoyed the pantomime awfully. I expect he'll tell the other chaps he saw me in a box with my trouser suit on. Do you think he noticed my trouser suit, Mother?'

But his mother hurled him into the car.

The drive home was George Knox's opportunity, and he delivered himself upon every topic of the day with violence and fluency, while Tony, who normally would have given his valueless views, sat in a dream. When they got to High Rising, George Knox got out first.

'Good God, Laura,' he said, anxiously fumbling about for the switch that turned on the inside lights. 'I have trodden on something human.'

He found the switch and light flooded the car. On the floor of the car lay a horrible dark-looking mess with pieces of something white sticking to it.

'Oh Mother, it's my mince-pie,' said Tony indignantly.

'What on earth did you want any more mince-pies for?' asked his exhausted mother.

'Mother, I didn't. It was for Rose, She couldn't have a treat, so I saved my other mince-pie for her and I had it in my school cap, but it must have fallen out.'

'Never mind, Tony,' said Dora, also in harmony with all the world. 'I won't tell Rose, and then she won't know.'

'Right-oh,' said Tony, 'then I'll eat it myself,' and

scooping the mangled mince-pie off the floor, he put it all into his mouth.

'Thanks awfully, sir,' he said to George Knox, his articulation much impeded by the squashed pie. 'It was a ripping show and it was frightful luck to see old Donk.'

And then he followed his mother into the house.

First published in Harper's Bazaar, *February 1935*

Christmas at Mulberry Lodge

William was six and Mary was about eight. They lived in London (which Mary knew was the capital of England but William was too little to know about capitals) in a very nice house with a garden, and it was so long ago that Queen Victoria was still reigning over England. Their nursery was up three pairs of stairs and there was a gate on the landing to keep them from coming down unless Nannie was with them or their mother sent for them. William boasted a great deal to Mary about how he would undo the gate and go downstairs when Nannie wasn't looking, but as a matter of fact he couldn't undo it at all because the latch was on the other side. Mary could easily reach over and undo it, but though she boasted a good deal to William about this, she never really did it because Nannie might have found out. Nannie was a rather sharp-nosed person, not very tall, but William and Mary thought her taller and more important than anyone in the world. If their mother told them to do anything, or not to do anything, they said, 'Oh Mother, need I?' But if Nannie gave an order they obeyed it at once. It was not that Nannie was unkind, but she knew exactly what was right and what was wrong for young ladies and gentlemen, and had a cousin called Albert who was a soldier and had once been allowed to come to tea in the nursery in a red coat before he went back to India. Besides these great advantages, Nannie said she had an eye in the back of her head that told her what William and Mary were doing when she had her back turned. William sometimes screamed after he had gone to bed because he said Nannie's eye was on the ceiling. Mary told him not to be so silly, but she really knew in the bottom of her heart that the reason Nannie wore high, stiff collars was so that no one should see where the eye lived. Otherwise, Nannie was very nice and used to sing hymns after tea by the nursery fire, before the gas was lighted, which gave the children a lovely sad feeling.

Every Christmas, William and Mary and Nannie with Mr and Mrs Mulberry (which was the name of the children's father and mother) went to the seaside where the old Mr and Mrs Mulberry lived, who were William and Mary's grandfather and grandmother. Old Mr and Mrs Mulberry had a large white house on the village green and two large prancing horses that came to the station with a carriage and a coachman and brought the whole family from the train to Mulberry Lodge, which was curiously enough the name of the house. William said it ought to be called Mulberry Bush, because of 'Here we go round the Mulberry Bush', and Mary said, 'Silly.' So William banged his toy drum and said, 'Mulberry Bush, Mulberry Bush,' again and again, and Mary got onto the rocking horse and rocked backwards and forwards shouting, 'Silly Billy, Silly Billy,' and the noise was quite dreadful, when suddenly Nannie, who had been down to the kitchen to get the milk and the butter for nursery tea, came into the room with them on a tray and said that was quite enough.

'But, Nannie,' said William, 'she said Silly Billy.'

'How often have I told you not to say "she",' said Nannie, putting the tray down. '"She" is the cat's grandmother, and don't let me have to tell you again and run along in the night nursery and wash your hands and put that drum away in the toy-cupboard at once.'

Mary was so pleased that she pointed at William and said a dreadful word, which was 'Idiot'. But Nannie, talking in a horrid voice and saying it all in one breath said How often had she told Miss Mary young ladies never pointed and if she said words like that to her brother she would have to tell her mother of her and to get down off the rocking horse at once and go and wash her hands for tea and if she hadn't dirtied her clean pinafore already and how all the packing was to be finished in time to go to Mulberry Lodge next day she couldn't think and if they made all that noise she couldn't ever get their stockings packed and then Father Christmas wouldn't give them any presents.

This was such a dreadful thought that William and Mary became perfectly quiet and ate their bread and butter, and their bread and jam (without butter), and two small rock cakes and a thick slice of chocolate cake each and said their grace and asked if they might get down. Then they washed their hands again, and William had his clean smock and Mary had a clean pinafore and they went down to the drawing-room to their mother. And Nannie packed and packed; and after they were in bed she packed and packed; and next morning, which was Christmas Eve, she packed and packed, till the whole family got into a four-wheeled cab drawn by a bony horse and went off to the station. And at about half-past twelve they got to the seaside and the two prancing horses with the carriage and the coachmen met them at the train and took them to Mulberry Lodge.

Now, the nursery at Mulberry Lodge was not very big, so Nannie and the children often had tea in the kitchen for a treat, and after tea Nannie had long conversations with Florence the parlour-maid about a cousin of Florence's who was in hospital and the children were allowed to go into the drawing-room till their bedtimes.

In the drawing-room they found a large white dust-sheet spread on the floor and on it a great heap of holly and ivy and mistletoe that the gardener had brought in that afternoon. Their father had a stepladder and was putting bits of holly along the tops of all the pictures. Their mother had a box of little nails and a hammer and was fastening ivy all round the door. Grandpapa was tying the mistletoe into bunches and told William to come and help him. Grandmamma had a little broom and a little dust-pan each with a long handle and was going about sweeping up all the leaves and berries that fell on the floor, and she told Mary to get the waste-paper basket and follow her, so that she could empty her little dustpan into it. Everyone worked very hard till half-past six when Nannie knocked at the door and came in.

'Now you must go to bed, darlings,' said their mother.

'Oh Mother, need we?' said William and Mary.

'Well, just five more minutes,' said their father. But Nannie, all in one breath, said She had just taken the bath water up and it was nice and hot and some people were quite excited enough already the sooner in bed the sooner it was day. William looked round for the excited people, but he couldn't see them anywhere, so he supposed Nannie must be seeing them out of the eye in the back of her head. Mary knew quite well that the sooner you were in bed the sooner it wasn't day at all, but night. But they both knew Nannie must be obeyed, so they said goodnight to the grown-ups and went upstairs, where Nannie gave them their bath in front of the nursery fire (for very few people had bathrooms when Queen Victoria was still Queen of England), and they each had a biscuit and a cup of warm milk and went to bed.

Now, every year they hung up their stockings on Christmas Eve, and every year since she was six Mary had tried to keep awake to see Father Christmas, and every year, which was two years, she had gone to sleep just before he came. Now, William used to sleep with Nannie at home, while Mary had a little room leading off their room to herself, but at Mulberry Lodge they slept together and Nannie had a room just across the passage and left her door and their door open all night so that she could hear them if they woke, but she snored so loudly that she could really hear nothing, and when once William and Mary had gone to sleep they never woke till time to get up.

But Christmas Eve is, as everyone knows, a rather special night, and William and Mary could not go to sleep. First there was the noise of the dressing gong. Then Florence looked in to say goodnight and give them each a ginger biscuit, Only not to tell Nannie. Then there was the dinner gong. By this time, of course, it was the middle of the night and William and Mary felt certain that Father Christmas would come at any moment, and then Mary's stocking and William's sock that were hanging so limp and empty at the end of their beds would be full of enchanting and interesting things done up in bright-coloured paper.

The fire was burning low now, and the gas (for hardly anyone had electric light when Queen Victoria was still Queen of England) was turned down so that they could only see a tiny blue flame.

'I shall stay awake all night,' said Mary.

'I shall stay awake all night too,' said William, who mostly copied Mary. But while they were staying awake all night a wonderful thing happened. First the big clock in the hall struck eight, which was later than anyone could imagine, and then very soft lovely music began to creep into the room. This was the waits, who were some of the village men that came round singing carols every year for shillings and sixpences, and every year Grandpapa said the noise was too dreadful and would Florence give them that shilling and tell them to go and sing outside Colonel Brown's house. And every year Grandmamma said they were doing their best and Florence must ask them into the kitchen and give them some beer and some cold pork-pie. As a matter of fact they were not doing their best, for all they did was to gabble through the carols as fast as possible and bang on the front door so that they could get a shilling and go on to Colonel Brown who sometimes gave them two shillings, and the noise was quite dreadful, but William and Mary in a warm room, with the window shut and their heads almost underneath the bedclothes, thought it was the loveliest noise they had ever heard and so went to sleep.

And now comes one of the really dreadful parts of the story.

Mary had been to sleep for hours and hours; in fact so long that the grown-ups had finished dinner and it was nearly nine o'clock, when Mother and Nannie came into the room.

'Shall I turn up the gas, m'm?' said Nannie.

'No, it might wake them,' said Mother. 'Light the candle and don't let it shine on their faces.'

So Nannie took a box of matches out of her apron pocket, because she never allowed William and Mary to have matches in their room in case they struck them and set the house on fire, and lighted a candle. And Mary, who was having a dream about her rocking-horse that he could gallop out of the nursery and away into the country, dreamed that she gave him a lump of sugar and he scrunched it up. And the striking of the match was just like the scrunch and she woke up and opened one eye. And just at that moment, Nannie moved the candle so that the light shone right into Mary's one open eye for a moment, and she opened the other. And what should she see but Mother and Nannie putting little parcels done up in bright-coloured paper into the stockings.

Now Mary knew in her secret self that Father Christmas wasn't exactly a real person, but she also knew that she mustn't say so and that William mustn't be told because he wasn't old enough. But to know a thing in your secret self is quite different from seeing Mother and Nannie filling your stockings, and Mary knew she ought to make a noise, or bounce about in bed, so that they would know she was awake and tiptoe away again. But she didn't. She shut her eyes tight and listened with all her ears, which was a dreadful thing to do.

Then she heard Nannie say to Mother, 'What a sweet little round thing, m'm. Won't it run away?'

And Mother, who was putting something into Mary's stocking, said, 'No, Nannie; it is quite cold.'

Then Mother put something on the chair by Mary's bed and went across to William's bed. Mary could hear her putting crackly paper things into William's sock and then she went round to the other side of his bed and put something on the chair beside him.

'Does it really go, m'm?' said Nannie.

'Of course,' said Mother in a laughing whisper. 'Their Aunt Isabel sent it.'

Then Nannie blew the candle out and she and Mother went away.

After this, Mary felt so full of naughtiness that she could hardly breathe. Also she wondered and wondered what it was that was cold and couldn't run away and what it was that really went. And she wondered so hard that she couldn't go to sleep at all. At least she quite well knew that she lay awake all night, but when she opened her eyes again Nannie was turning the gas up and it was a dark, cold Christmas morning and half-past seven o'clock.

'Happy Christmas!' said William and Mary at the tops of their voices.

'Happy Christmas, I'm sure!' said Nannie. 'Now put on your dressing-gowns and slippers and you can take your stockings into Grandmamma's room.'

William and Mary both screamed with pleasure and got up and began to put on their dressing-gowns and slippers. Mary had one arm in her dressing-gown when she saw on the chair by her bed a little cage. It was rather long and not very high and at one end of it was a wooden box with a little round hole in it. Over the hole was a little wooden shutter that could be pulled up and down, so that anyone who lived in the cage could go into the box when the shutter was up, but not when it was down. On the top of the wooden box was a lid with a little hook. Mary unfastened the hook and opened the lid. Inside the box was a charming nest made of hay and dry moss, but there was no one in the nest and no one in the cage.

'I can put my little china owl called Rudolph in the nest,' said Mary.

Nannie said Never mind about owls and to run along into Grannie's room and take the cage and the stocking with her and see what happened.

Then William who had put one foot into his bedroom slipper suddenly stood as still as a snowman for on the chair by his bed was a little clock, ticking away and saying twenty-five minutes to eight.

'Oh!!!' said William. 'Does it really go?'

'Of course it does,' said Mary; and she nearly said, 'because Aunt Isabel sent it,' but her secret self remembered that she ought not to have been awake last night, so she said nothing and put her other arm into her dressing-gown and went down the passage to Grannie's room, carrying her stocking and her cage, while William, with both his bedroom slippers on, came after her with his sock and his clock.

In Grannie's room a bright fire was already burning and everything smelled of lavender water. William and Mary climbed onto Grannie's large four-poster bed with muslin curtains and said, 'A Happy Christmas,' and snuggled under the eiderdown, one on each side of Grannie, to show her their presents. They both talked at once so Grannie said, 'William first, because he is the smallest.'

William was so excited that he could hardly speak, especially as one of his front teeth was very loose, so he held the clock up and said, 'It goes.'

'How lovely,' said Grannie. And she showed him how to wind it up.

'Every night you must wind it up till it feels stiff,' said Grannie. 'But when it feels stiff, don't wind any more, or you will break it. And now what is in your stocking?'

Perhaps the things in William's stocking will not seem

very amusing to you, but when Queen Victoria was still Queen of England they were all that heart could desire. They were

A humming top that sang a lovely sad note and would change to another note if you hit it hard while it was spinning
A little bag of button chocolates with tiny white sugar balls on them
A mouth organ
A book of transfers
A real pocket-knife with two blades
A box of coloured chalks
A Plate Lifter, which was a rubber bulb with a long rubber tube and a little rubber bag at the end of it. If you put the little bag under somebody's plate at dinner and then squeezed the bulb, the plate jumped about
And right at the bottom, in the toe, a tangerine orange

'Now, said Grannie to Mary, 'we will look at your presents.'

'First I have a lovely cage,' said Mary. 'I shall put my china owl called Rudolph in it.'

Grannie smiled in a rather mysterious way but said nothing.

Then Mary began to empty her stocking. In it she found

A handkerchief with M in one corner
A little fruit-knife with a mother o' pearl handle
and a silver blade
A very small prayer book in such tiny print that
no one could read it and some angel children's
heads stamped in silver on the cover
A thimble
A very tiny bottle of eau de Cologne
and
A little brooch made of forget-me-nots

And at the bottom was something cold.

'A tangerine like William's,' said Mary. 'We always get tangerines in our stockings.' She put her hand in and pulled it out.

But it wasn't a tangerine.

It was small and brown and furry.

It was curled up into a ball and its tiny hands were over its sharp little face.

'Oh! It's a mouse!' said Mary. 'Oh, how darling! It's still asleep, Grannie, I'll wake it up!'

'It is a dormouse,' said Grannie. 'You mustn't wake it, because it has to sleep all winter. Put it in the nest in the wooden box and it will be quite happy there, and when spring comes it will wake up and come out of the little wooden box into the cage and run about, and you can feed it with hazelnuts and walnuts and hemp and bits of apple, and give it clean sand in its house every day.'

So Mary put the dormouse into the nest of hay and dry moss and fastened the hook and then she and William went back to their room and got dressed.

'Wasn't the dormouse a nice surprise?' said Nannie, while she was tying Mary's hair with a blue bow.

'Not a surprise,' said Mary, 'because I knew I was going to have it.'

'You couldn't,' said Nannie. 'Father only brought it back from the shop yesterday and stand still while I do your bow.'

Then Mary felt wicked again in her secret self, because truly she could never have known about the dormouse unless she had done that dreadful thing of being awake last night. Of course she hadn't known that it was a dormouse, but she did know it was something round and cold and perhaps now Nannie would know how naughty she had been. So she said nothing.

There were sausages for breakfast because of Christmas Day and more presents and the whole family went to church. William wanted to take all his presents, but Nannie said only heathen little boys took toys to church, or chalks, or transfers, or chocolates, or tangerines, and he could play with them all when he came back. So he took his new pocket-knife with two blades, and when Nannie wasn't looking he put his Plate Lifter in his pocket as well.

Nannie let Mary sprinkle some of her eau de Cologne on her handkerchief and pin her forget-me-not brooch on her frock and the little prayer book of course went to church with her. But while Nannie was buttoning William's gaiters, Mary did quite a dreadful thing, even worse than pretending she was asleep when she wasn't. She opened the cage and took the dormouse out of his nest and put him in her pocket with her handkerchief.

All through the service Mary was thinking about her dormouse, and whenever she wasn't using her little prayer book she put her hand in her pocket to feel how it was getting on, and every time she thought it felt a little warmer; but she couldn't be quite sure. Presently she took one of her gloves off so that she could feel better, but Nannie, who was sitting a pew behind, said Take your hand out of your pocket and put on your glove again at once and in church too, Miss Mary, so she put it on again in a great hurry and was so afraid that Nannie would ask why she was putting her hand in her pocket that she was afraid to take her handkerchief out, and sniffed. Nannie said in a dreadful whisper Not to sniff in church and to get her handkerchief out at once. Mary was afraid that Nannie would reach over and get the handkerchief out herself, but most luckily William behaved very badly just then. He was tired of being at church and sitting on a hard seat with his short legs swinging in the air, so he had taken his Plate Lifter out of his pocket and slipped one end under Grandmamma's prayer book and squeezed the bulb. The prayer book gave a jump and Grandmamma put on her spectacles to see what was happening, but as quick as lightning Nannie, who must have had eyes all over her head as well as her usual two and the one at the back, reached over from the pew behind and took the Plate Lifter out of William's hand and put it in her pocket. William was so surprised that he was as good as gold for the rest of the service and Mary was as good as gold too.

When they got back Nannie said to come upstairs and wash their hands before lunch, and now something had happened more dreadful than anything that had happened yet. Mary was just going to take her coat off, but she thought she would feel if the dormouse was still there, so she put her hand in her pocket. Something very warm and wriggly was there. She took out her hand with the dormouse in it. The dormouse sat up for half a second and looked at her with his bright eyes and then he sprang out of her hand onto the floor, rushed away like a flash of lightning and was out of the door and down the passage before anyone could stop him.

Mary began to cry at the top of her voice, which was very loud indeed. William was so excited that he began to cry too, and they made such a noise that their father and mother came rushing up to see what had happened.

'Oh Mother, Mother,' yelled Mary, 'I only wanted to take my dormouse to church and he has woken up and run away.' And she made such a noise that Grandfather and Grandmother came up too. And when anyone could hear themselves speak, Grandmother said she had told Mary that the dormouse must be left in its nest till it woke up, and Mary yelled more than ever, and was so unhappy that she told her mother all about her wickedness last night and how she had really been awake all the time, but she was crying and sniffing so much that no one could really hear what she said. So her mother hugged her and said Never mind and to wash her face before lunch.

When one has cried a great deal and yelled and bellowed one often feels much better, and Mary was very good all that afternoon. William was not quite so good, because he had to use his new pocket-knife with two blades and he cut a hole in the nursery tablecloth.

When bath-time came they were both very tired and sleepy. Nannie had put the water into the bath and came down to the drawing-room to fetch them. They said goodnight to everyone and climbed upstairs to the nursery. Before the fire was the bath, and the towels were hanging on the fender, getting nice and warm. Mary was just going to take her frock off when she saw something in the bath. It was a little brown thing, floating on the water.

'Nannie! Nannie!' she said.

Nannie, who had just come in with their biscuit and milk for supper, looked in the bath.

'There now, it's your dormouse, Miss Mary,' she said. 'Grannie told you to leave it in its nest and now the poor little thing has got into the bath and got drowned. I'll get it out and don't dawdle now or the water will get cold.'

'Nannie,' said William.

'That's enough, Master William,' said Nannie, 'and you can't have that Plate Lifter tonight, but if you are good I'll see if I'll let you have it tomorrow, and don't you start crying again, Miss Mary, because crying doesn't do no good.'

'Nannie,' said William.

'That's *enough*, Master William,' said Nannie. 'And if you don't stop crying, Miss Mary, you'll have to go to bed at once without your biscuit.'

'Nannie,' said William, who always went on till he got what he wanted, 'can we have a funeral for the dormouse tomorrow?'

And when Mary heard this lovely suggestion she quite forgot to cry and Nannie put the poor dormouse into a cardboard box with some cotton wool over it to wait till the funeral. Then William and Mary had a quick bath and ate their supper.

'Don't you want to wind up your clock, Master William?' said Nannie, as the children were getting into bed.

'No,' said William.

'No what?' said Nannie.

'No, thank you,' said William. 'It said it didn't want to be wound up tonight.'

Nannie said that was nonsense and began winding it up herself, but the handle went round and round and the clock didn't wind.

'Have you been winding the clock, Master William?' said Nannie.

William got right under the bedclothes and said nothing, so everyone knew he had disobeyed Grandmamma and wound it up till it broke.

'You *are* a naughty boy,' said Nannie, but not very angrily, because she was quite tired with all the naughty things William and Mary had done on Christmas Day. Then she tucked them up and said goodnight and took the clock away. And in ten minutes both the children were fast asleep.

Of course, in a proper story people who let their dormouses wake up and run away and get drowned and other people who used their Plate Lifters in church and broke their clocks would come to a dreadful end. But in their story there are no dreadful ends. Mary was very sorry that she had behaved so badly, and William was very sorry that Nannie had seen him playing with his Plate Lifter and had noticed that his clock was broken, but next day Nannie gave him the Plate Lifter back and the clock was mended by Mr Clamp the watchmaker in the village. Only, for a punishment, William had to learn to tell the time.

As for the dormouse, it had a lovely funeral and was buried under the apple tree after lunch. And what is more, their father drew a picture of the dormouse flying over the garden with wings and Mary coloured it with William's chalks, all except the purple one which he wouldn't let her use, but as she didn't really want it she didn't much mind. And Grandfather had the picture framed in a beautiful gold frame and it was hung in the nursery.

'And what will that always remind you of, Miss Mary?' said Nannie, in a rather important voice.

Of course she meant Mary to say it would remind her of how naughty she had been.

But Mary and William both said, 'The Funeral.'

And if you look in Mr and Mrs Mulberry's house in London, I believe you will find the picture of the dormouse still hanging in Mary's mother's bedroom.

First published in The Shining Tree and Other Christmas Stories, *1940*

St Valentine's Holiday

Tony Morland's school had an arrangement, agreeable to masters and boys, devastating to parents, by which the boarders could go home for the weekend three times in the term. Early in February, Laura Morland received the following letter from her son:

DEAR MOTHER, –

Please can I come home for the weekend that has February the 14th in it. This is most important. I had to go to some beastly kind of concert on Friday and Fairweather threw paper darts at a chap and got whacked. More when we meet.

Your loving son

Tony.

P.S.– Please could you get me some new grey flannel trousers because a boy called Pidloe (C. J. St. P.) had been burning the edge of the prep-room fender with a red-hot poker and when I sat on it it was still smoldering. Also my pyjamas have split across the back again and matron says they arnt worth mending. Could I have a 9d. packet of stamp hinges. This is urgent.

Laura, who was weak enough to hate disappointing her demon child, did as she was told, and on the Friday afternoon drove over to Tony's school. It was bitterly cold, and Laura's temper was not improved by the thought that she would have to drive that very road again on Sunday evening to take Tony back, but when she saw her youngest son with a clean, serious face, his weekend bag in his hand, a large muffler round his neck, waiting for her on the school steps, her heart leapt.

'Have you got the stamp hinges, Mother?' asked Tony. 'Oh, good on you. Mother, can we stop at Stoke Dry? I've got some important shopping to do.'

'Yes, if the shops are still open. Where's your overcoat?'

'Oh Mother, need I have an overcoat? I've got my muffler.'

'That's neither here nor there,' said Laura, with surprising firmness. 'Get your overcoat at once, and your gloves. It's freezing hard.'

Tony went unwillingly into the boarding house, and after a very long interval emerged, carrying his coat with as much difficulty as Christian carried his burden.

'Put it on,' said Laura.

'Oh Mother—'

'Put your coat on at once, Morland,' said matron, appearing behind him. 'Good evening, Mrs Morland. Did Morland tell you about his grey trousers? That was Pidloe's fault. Really, Mrs Morland, the boys seem to be particularly troublesome this term. Neither to hold nor to bind as they say. Syrup of Figs all round is what they need. Your lad isn't like the rest, Mrs Morland,' said matron, patting Tony on the shoulder, at which he winced and cast up his eyes to heaven. 'He's quite a little help to me. When Pussy was so ill he was quite concerned.'

Before matron could get her second wind and embark upon the saga of her bad leg and her married sister's little girl in Bournemouth, Laura had excused herself on grounds of lateness, said goodbye and driven off.

'Who is Pussy?' she asked.

'Pussy? Oh, *Pussy*. Matron's cat. It got its paw in the prep-room door when Donk was being Horatius, and I went to cheer it up. I have a kind of instinct about animals, Mother. I held its paw, and it looked at me with grateful eyes.'

Wrapped in a dream of his own noble philanthropy, Tony sat silent till they reached the outskirts of Stoke Dry. Here the shining lights in the shop windows roused him to life.

'Mother, could we stop at Woolworth's?' he asked.

'All right, Tony, but be quick. I can't park here long.'

'I know. Mother, do you think I could have my next week's pocket-money now? I need it rather importantly. Oh, thanks awfully, Mother.'

Before the Stoke Dry policeman, who was a friend of Laura's, had warned her more than twice, Tony came back with a long parcel, and they drove on towards High Rising.

'Mother,' said Tony, 'can you guess what I was getting? I was getting some red crêpe paper and some gold ink to make Valentines. I thought Rose and Dora would like Valentines, and Stoker. I shall cut out red hearts and stick them on cardboard. Have you any cardboard, Mother? About roughly nine by six. White cardboard, I mean, not cardboard-box kind of cardboard. I'll make you a Valentine, too, if you'd like.'

'Thank you, Tony, I'd love one. I've still got that poem you sent me from school for a Valentine about two years ago.'

'I know. And I'll make one for Mr and Mrs Knox and Mr Knox's Annie. I did think of making one for Mrs Coates's baby, but I don't think she would appreciate it, as she's so small.'

By this time they had reached the house, and Laura told her son to hurry up and get washed for supper while she put the car away. She found Tony waiting for her in the dining-room and Stoker bringing in their meal.

'Shepherd's pie! Oh, good on you, Stoker,' said Tony.

'Stoker, do you want a Valentine? I'm going to make Valentines for Rose and Dora, and I'll make you one too. Mother, could I have some cardboard and your scissors and the Stickphast? I shall have to work frightfully hard because of Sunday being St Valentine's Day. Would you really like a Valentine, Stoker?'

'Don't mind if I do,' said Stoker. 'I suppose you've heard they got him round,' she added to Laura.

'Got who round?'

'That Sid Brown.'

'Round what?'

'Round again. Showing off to Mr Knox's Annie, that's what it was, and it took two men and a rope, silly young fellow. Mr Mallow at the station was properly wild, with the weekend traffic coming on and Dr Ford saying young Sid was to have Saturday off.'

'What *are* you talking about, Stoker?'

'Anyone with any sense in their heads would have known the ice wasn't bearing yesterday, and of course that Sid Brown had to go skating round Rising Mere because it was Mr Knox's Annie's afternoon off, and so he fell in near the weir, and it's the mercy of Providence his poor mother isn't wearing mourning for him at this very moment. Then there was that sheep got drowned down at the weir last Sunday. They say there's always three of everything, so we've more troubles to come. And the butcher says there isn't no lamb's fry, so—'

'Oh Mother!' interrupted Tony, who had been listening with glistening eyes to this village tragedy. 'Oh Mother, can I skate? I greased my skates when I put them away. Oh Mother, can I? I've never skated on real ice, only on a rink. Mother, I bet I'd simply whoosh round the Mere.'

'Do you want to fall in and be drowned like Sid Brown?' asked his mother, rather hoping to dissuade him from this treat.

'Take more than that to drown Sid, nor Master Tony neither,' said Stoker. 'Ice is bearing all right today. Mrs Mallow tells me Dr Ford was all over the Mere after tea. Shouldn't wonder if I went on the slide myself. Worlsing on the ice is what I like. My cousin, the one that got knocked down by the car the day her husband came out of the hospital, was a lovely worlser. Hazeline her name was. Master Tony won't come to no harm.'

Laura as usual could not resist and said that Tony might skate, provided Dr Ford said it was safe, and Rose and Dora went with him. What with skates and Valentines, Tony's conversation became so intolerable that his mother packed him off to bed at half-past eight. At half-past nine he was still in his bath. At ten o'clock his mother shouted up to him to be quiet, and five minutes later, when she went up herself, she found him heavily asleep, his skating boots with well-Vaselined skates tucked under his pillow. She withdrew them, observing with some disfavour the mingled stains of blacking and Vaseline on the sheets, kissed her son's warm pink cheek and went to bed.

After telephoning to Dr Ford and Mrs Gould the Vicar's wife, skating was arranged for two o'clock on Saturday afternoon. Mrs Gould said that Rose and Dora had a French girl staying with them till Monday, a pupil at the school where her elder daughter was games mistress, and she hoped Tony would come back to tea. On hearing of a French girl, Tony became remote, and retired upstairs with his red paper and golden ink, all the cardboard Laura and Stoker could find, a pot of Stickphast and Laura's large scissors. With these Laura found him still busily engaged at lunch-time.

'Oh Mother,' he cried reproachfully, 'You've looked.'

'I really didn't, Tony. I only saw something red.'

'That's Stoker's Valentine. I drew a picture of her and I cut out a lot of red hearts and stuck them all over her and wrote "Valentine, Cook Divine" under it. Do you think she'll like it, Mother?'

'I'm sure she will. Now wipe some of that paste off your hands and face and come down to lunch.'

In the highest spirits, only slightly damped by his mother's heartless insistence that he should wear his overcoat, Tony set out for Rising Mere, a little lake made by a low dam across the Rising, with a weir at one side. The lake was known to be shallow, except near the weir, a fact which just enabled Laura to bear up against her usual premonitions of evil and Stoker's prophecy of a third disaster. The vicarage party were already on the bank.

'This is Françoise, Tony,' said Mrs Gould. 'She is fourteen, just older than Rose, and she skates beautifully.'

'Hullo, Tony,' said Dora. 'Françoise talks English, so you needn't be afraid.'

A more tactless introduction could hardly have been made. Tony scowled heavily at Dora and stuck out a hand at Françoise, who instantly wrung it so hard as to enforce Tony's unwilling admiration.

'She's got a jolly good grip anyway,' said he to Rose and Dora, feeling it safer not to address Françoise personally.

'What does he say I have?' asked Françoise.

The confusion between grip and *grippe* having been cleared up, the three elder children began to put on their skates. Tony's idea of a French girl, founded on his early and unwilling studies of *Les Malheurs de Sophie*, was of a dark, frizzly-haired little being in wide skirts and pantalettes. He was therefore considerably relieved to find Françoise a perfectly ordinary girl of about his own size, in dress and appearance quite like Rose and Dora. He was further relieved to hear her talking perfectly good English, and his unspoken fear that he might have so far to disgrace himself as to say something in French vanished.

'I say, those are decent boots of yours,' said Tony, looking at Françoise's high, beautifully cut skating boots.

'All the best skaters at St Moritz have these boots,' said Françoise. 'I skate at St Moritz every winter. You should have boots like these. They have *beaucoup de chic*.'

'So has Tony,' said Dora, '*beaucoup de cheek*.'

This ill-timed levity fell flat. Tony looked witheringly, and Rose reprovingly, at Dora, who, not a whit abashed, jumped up and down in a very annoying way. The three elder children then went on to the ice and Tony fell down.

'Hullo, my boy,' said Dr Ford, swooping down on them. 'Don't do that. I'm taking an afternoon off. No broken legs or arms today, because I shan't mend them. Here, Françoise, come round with me.'

He swung Françoise off to the middle of the Mere, where they gave a brilliant exhibition of fancy skating.

'I expect you'd like to go round the edge,' said Tony to Rose as he picked himself up. 'I daresay you're a bit out of practice. I don't know how it is, but I don't get out of practice. I suppose it's a kind of gift that I have.'

As he spoke, he propelled himself laboriously along the edge of the Mere, his body curiously bent, his arms flourishing. Rose skated quietly by his side, while Dora went off to the slides, where such village children as had escaped their mothers' annoying way of finding Saturday afternoon jobs for them were rushing about with loud screams.

'It's all a question of balance,' said Tony. 'You see, people have something in their ears that makes them balance, and if they haven't got it, they can't balance at all. I have a kind of balance without taking any trouble. Can you do edges?'

'A little,' said Rose.

'There's a chap at school,' said Tony, clutching at Rose to steady himself, 'who does edges. I went to the rink with him and he did edges like anything, and the instructor told him to get out the middle and not be a silly young ass.'

'Oh Tony,' said Rose, admiringly.

The short winter afternoon passed quickly. Françoise and Dr Ford amused themselves together. Tony, accompanied by Rose, who could have easily deserted him for more skilful companions, plodded steadily about near the bank. The slide was patronised by Dora, and later by Stoker, who, with loud coy shrieks, was pushed and pulled along by Sid Brown, miraculously well enough to be on the ice, and Mr Reid of the shop. Upon them, Dr Ford suddenly descended and ordered Sid Brown to go home.

'Off you go,' he shouted, taking off his boots, 'or you'll get me in trouble with the B.M.A. Tony, Rose, come off the ice. I'm going to drive you all home. Come here, Dora. Get your boots off, Françoise. My God, I'm stiff.'

'I'm never stiff, sir,' said Tony politely. 'I suppose I have a kind of natural unstiffness. Some of the chaps get awfully stiff when they start gym after the holidays, but I don't. You ought to keep your muscles well exercised, sir. If you did muscle exercises—'

'Shut up,' said Dr Ford.

'Hurry up, all of you,' said Mrs Gould as she opened the Vicarage door. 'Daddy is waiting for his tea. Wash as fast as you can.'

The girls were soon back, but Tony lingered unaccountably. When he entered the dining-room his hair was wetly plastered to his head and dripping gently on to his jacket.

'Sit down, Tony. What have you been doing?' asked Mrs Gould. The Vicar, never a friend of Tony's, looked unkindly at him.

'I had to do my hair, Mrs Gould,' said Tony, 'and Mr Gould doesn't have any brilliantine. I suppose it really isn't much use for him, so I had to put water on my hair. You ought to get some Floral Solidified Brilliantine, sir,' said Tony, passing a plate of scones to the Vicar so crookedly that they all slid off on to the table. 'You can get it for threepence at Woolworth's. I always use it, it's awfully good. There's a master at school called Mr Prothero, and he's getting bald and he uses it.'

'Am I to say grace or not, Dorothea?' asked the Vicar of his wife in a voice of priestly irritation.

'Yes, dear,' replied Mrs Gould. 'Dora, pick those scones

up and scrape that butter off the tablecloth with your knife. No, a clean knife; and use it flat, Dora; FLAT, I said.'

'I'll do it,' said Tony, leaning across Dora. 'You ought to have a palette knife. Mr Atkins, who teaches drawing at school, has a palette knife, and when Pidloe upset all the jam at tea, Mr Atkins scraped it all off with his palette knife and it hardly showed at all.'

The Vicar pushed back his chair and left the room.

'Rose,' said Mrs Gould, quite unperturbed, 'take Daddy a cup of tea in his study. Tony, go on with your tea. Dora, don't giggle. Françoise, some more cake?'

'And what did you do this afternoon, Tony?' asked Françoise, evidently feeling that she ought to help to slur over a discreditable episode. 'I did not see you. Dr Ford skates with *beaucoup de chic*.'

'So does Tony,' said Dora.

Tony glowered at Dora.

'I was doing edges,' he said with some truth. 'Dora was only sliding.'

'Ah, edges,' said Françoise. 'Have you been to France?'

'Yes,' said Tony, 'I went to Dieppe for the day with Mr and Mrs Knox and we were all sick and I went to a French cinema and had some wine.'

'And what film did you see?' pursued Françoise, perhaps a shade condescendingly.

'*Mickey Mouse* and the *Three Little Pigs*.'

'The *Three Little Pigs* is English,' said Dora.

Tony, with a fine effort of courage – for to quell Dora might at the same time disgrace him in the eyes of Françoise, who wore long boots and skated at St Moritz – fixed Dora with a coldly hostile eye, and remarked with a very passable accent, '*Qui craint le grand méchant loup?*'

'Ah, but he speaks French perfectly, your friend,' said Françoise.

Tony, his position thus established, rapidly formed a bosom friendship with Françoise, which consisted chiefly in giggling together and snubbing Rose and Dora, but Dora the irrepressible skirmished round them and harassed their conversation, till Tony, intoxicated with social success, again hazarded his reputation.

'*Elle est mal élevée*,' he remarked with as careless an air as he could assume.

'*Ah, quant à mal élevée, je ne dis pas ça*,' said Françoise, looking expressively at Mrs Gould. '*Elle est plutôt enfantine. Quand je vous dis, Tony*—' And to Tony's horror she burst into a cascade of rapid French. He would undoubtedly have been exposed, had not the Vicar come in.

'Who left the tap on in the cloakroom?' he enquired.

'The tap, sir? Oh, the *tap*. Well, sir, I didn't leave it running, but I turned it on again to get my comb wet so that I could do my hair, and it must have stayed on.'

Mrs Gould then sent Tony home.

*

At supper his mother found him strangely silent, and his behaviour under the strain of being read aloud to was irreproachable. Laura, going up to kiss him in bed, found him studying a French grammar.

'Would you say I could talk decent French, Mother?' he asked.

'School French. If you went abroad you'd soon talk. Did you talk French to Françoise at all?'

'A bit,' said Tony, going bright scarlet, which his mother, folding his suit, did not see. 'Mother, I've made a Valentine for Françoise. Would you like to see it?'

From under his pillow he pulled a card covered with red hearts, gold paint, paste and dirty finger marks. Under the hearts was written the legend *Valentine, Reine des Patines*.

'It's a poem,' said Tony. 'Will she understand it, do you think?'

'Well, Tony, *patines* doesn't exactly mean skates, of course.'

'I know. But I expect she has enough sense to know it's a poem.'

On Sunday afternoon the children met again at the Mere. While Françoise was moving to join Dr Ford, Tony, fired with love and ambition, approached her, followed by Dora.

'I bet I can waltz,' he said to Françoise. 'Come on and

try. I've made a lovely Valentine specially for you. It's in my pocket and you can have it when we go back to tea.'

'I bet you can't waltz,' said Dora, giving him a hard shove.

Tony threw up his arms, slid wildly across the ice, and crashed into Françoise as she was pirouetting. Both children came heavily down in a windmill of arms and legs.

'I only lost my balance for a moment,' said Tony, sitting up.

'Clumsy English pig,' cried Françoise. She then burst into tears and smacked his face.

'That's enough, Françoise,' said Dr Ford, removing her with an iron hand.

Tony went back to the bank in perfect silence and took off his boots. Rose and Dora, shocked witnesses of the scene, stood in sympathetic silence.

'Here, Rose and Dora,' said Tony with an effort, 'I've made these Valentines for you. You are the only people except Stoker and Mother that I bothered to make them for.'

The girls were profuse in admiration and thanks. Tony's seared spirits began to revive, and his cure was completed by a rowdy half-hour on the slides with his village friends. Dr Ford, who had to visit a patient at some distance, offered to take Tony back to school, an offer which Laura gratefully accepted.

'Goodbye, darling,' said his mother. 'Did you have a nice French talk with Françoise?'

'She isn't much use,' said Tony loftily. 'I shouldn't think she knows any really important things in French. I asked her what gauge the French railways were, and she didn't know.'

Laura, a little puzzled by Tony's sudden want of interest in the French girl, went up to his play-room to tidy it, and incidentally to look for her large scissors. After a prolonged search she discovered them in the waste-paper basket. Among fragments of red paper and cardboard, looking suspiciously like a Valentine, the draft of an unfinished letter in Tony's hand caught her eye.

'*Chère Françoise*,' she read, '*vous êtes un sot—*'

It appeared to Laura that her son's first love affair was over.

First published in Harper's Bazaar, *February 1936*

High Voltage at Low Rising

One fine morning in April, George Knox, the celebrated biographer, was working in his library at Low Rising. The well-known author was dressed for the part in a blue flannel shirt, bedroom slippers, and a very peculiar suit consisting of loose trousers, wide at the ankle like a sailor's, and a braided pea-jacket, both made of a material not unlike the fur of a Teddy Bear. Several pipes lay on the table. He held between his clenched teeth another pipe, very large and of rugged appearance, which he was vainly endeavouring to light. Vainly, because however many matches a celebrated writer strikes, it is impossible to relight a pipe that has no tobacco in it. George Knox's sparse hair, which needed cutting, was all standing on end owing to the number of times he had run his pencil through it, and the knobs on his forehead were glistening with literary effort. Before him lay sheets of paper covered with his beautiful flowing handwriting, and with so many alterations and erasures that they had more the look of an arabesque than of a manuscript.

A knock at the door made him call out, 'Come in,' in a voice of patient irritation. His wife Anne half opened the door and, standing in the doorway, said, 'George, Laura is coming up the drive. Do you want to see her?'

George Knox stared at his wife, as at an unknown object several hundred miles away. Gradually his gaze focused itself, the light of reason returned to his eyes, and his pipe fell out of his mouth. He stooped to pick it up, but it had fallen under the table and he was obliged to contort his large frame in an alarming way to reach it.

'My dear Anne,' said his voice from under the table, while a leg and a left arm flourished in the air in his effort to balance, 'come in and shut the door. How often have I begged, nay, implored you to consider the title of that delightful *chef d'oeuvre* of the romantic, and yet it hardly falls under the category of romantic, yet still less under that of classical school, though heaven knows the life of the author, persecuted and badgered as he was by that male impersonator, that trousered virago, George Sand, a devourer of men if ever there was one, a female, if she may be called, repellent in every sense, yet not, my dear Anne,' said George Knox, his face, red but satisfied, appearing again above the table, while his right hand grasped the pipe, 'not without genius, if it were only for the incredible length of her works, the life of the author,

I say, was in a way the epitome of the romance, though how one is to distinguish between *Elle et Lui* and *Lui et Elle*, I have never yet discovered—'

'It doesn't matter, George,' said Anne. 'All I want to know at present is if you want to see Laura or not.'

'Laura? But what has she to do with the subject we, or rather, I, were or was discussing? I was merely, when my pipe, with that devilish liveliness peculiar to inanimate and senseless objects, chose to leap from me and caused me to grovel in a way unbecoming to my age, besides making all the blood fly to my head, I was, as I say, begging you, my dear Anne, nay, imploring you to remember, to bear in mind while memory holds a seat in this distracted globe, not that your head, my dear, is globular, on the contrary it is a very pretty oval shape, *omne vivum ex ovo*, and indeed I may say well that all my happiness, all my health, any slight game that I may have won, comes from you, to remember, I say, the title of the little *chef d'oeuvre* by the author of *Fantasio*, whose name even now trembles on my lips, do not interrupt me, Anne, for well do I know to whom I refer, though my ageing and palsied mind refuses to respond as once it did and no longer can I bend the bow of Odysseus – you know very well whom I mean, Anne,' said George Knox angrily.

While he was still speaking, Laura Morland appeared at the French window, tapped on it, found it shut, waved her hand, disappeared and almost immediately reappeared in the room.

'In trouble again, George?' said Laura, twisting up a few odds and ends of hair and pushing them under her hat.

George Knox rolled about in his seat like Dr Johnson, preparatory to speaking, but was forestalled by his wife, who said to Laura:

'George has to do a talk for the B.B.C., Laura, about Milton, and he can't think how to begin. I've got to go to the village, so do stay with him and help him. Is Tony with you?'

'He did come with me,' said Laura, looking vaguely about, 'but I expect he went round to the kitchen. Oh, no, there he is in the willow tree. I know he'll fall off into the pond, and if it is deep he will be drowned, and if it is shallow he will suffocate in the mud. Which is it?'

'I'll tell him to come in,' said Anne, soothingly. 'And I'll tell them to bring in some tea and cakes and you can have a good long talk.'

Laura saw her hostess cross the lawn and shout to Tony, who on hearing of cakes came down at once, though by as uncomfortable a route and one as much calculated to alarm his mother as possible, winding up with a sketch of falling into the pond, a loud shriek and a jump to earth. After a moment's conversation with Anne, he arrived at the library door, opened it halfway and stood there, looking injured.

'Mother,' said Tony, '*need* I come in? I was just going to show you a new way to climb the willow. You remember the way I climbed it last summer, Mr Knox, getting up by the low branch. Well, that branch was rotten and it broke off, so I invented an awfully good new way. First you get on the boat-house roof—'

'No, you do not,' cried George Knox. 'That roof is made of some material nameless to me, but fragile in the extreme, not calculated to withstand—'

'It's three-ply, sir, with asbestos on it, and tarred all over the outside,' said Tony kindly. 'It's absolutely safe, so you needn't worry. Besides, even if I did go through it, it would only be one leg, and I'd easily get out. Donk and I went on the roof of the bicycle shed at school last term and—'

'What do I care for what you and your friend with the un-Christian name, that sphinx in whom silence probably conceals total vacuity, did last term?' cried George Knox, 'You may both fall through all the bicycle sheds in Christendom, an expression, I admit, my dear Laura, perhaps tautologous when you consider how lately I had used the word un-Christian, though tautologous is not exactly the expression I meant, for though I long ago – not with pride, Laura, not with pride do I say this, but in all humility – lapsed from the Catholic Church to which my mother, herself necessarily as devout Frenchwoman being *croyante*, not to say *pratiquante*, doomed me; though I long ago fell away from the Mother of Churches, an expression indefinitely preferable, my dear Laura, to the Scarlet Woman, or the Whore of Babylon, not that I would ever use either; this lapse, I say, does not make me unconscious that the two words Christendom and un-Christian cannot be considered as identical, so that the question of tautology does not arise; but I wander, I become confused . . .'

George Knox groaned and tried to light his pipe again.

'You can't light it, sir, unless you put some tobacco in it,' said Tony.

George Knox's spirit was too broken to do anything but groan again.

'Tony, eat those cakes and look at a book or something,' said his mother. 'It's all right, George, you aren't mad, only talking too much. One often says a word that's like another word because the first word reminds you of another word that's like it, and then you say it. At least I often do. When is this talk about Milton that you're doing?'

'On Easter Tuesday,' said George Knox firmly, 'I fight with beasts at Ephesus.'

'If you mean you are talking on the wireless on Easter Tuesday, George,' said Laura, handing him a cup of tea, 'say so.'

'One might make a kind of joke about beasts and the B.B.C.,' said Tony. 'Something about the B. Beast C., or the Beast B. C.'

'One mightn't,' snapped George Knox.

'Sir,' continued Tony, disregarding these unkind words, 'can I listen to you talking? Oh Mother, can we listen to Mr Knox talking? We'll have the new wireless fixed then. Oh Mother, can we? I'd love to hear you on the wireless, sir. Will it be National or Regional? There's going to be a conference this year about wavelengths. The Droitwich wavelength is too powerful so that it cuts in on all sorts of interesting things. I daresay you've noticed that, sir. There are a lot of foreign stations that you can't get, because of Droitwich cutting in on them. Shall I show you, sir? I can find practically any foreign station without knowing the wavelength. It's a kind of instinct I have, I suppose.'

As he spoke, and without waiting for an answer, Tony went over to George Knox's wireless set and turned it on. By a deft manipulation of the knobs he produced from the instrument a succession of wails, hoots, bangs, crackles and sounds as of a distant dance band of demons.

'Don't do that, Tony,' said his mother, eyeing her son's complacent face with some irritation.

'But, Mother, that *shows*. What you need, sir,' he continued, addressing George Knox, 'is a super het. It wouldn't cost an awful lot, and it would cut out all that sort of thing. It's all to do with electricity and you wouldn't understand it, especially if I explained it, but a super het gets the wavelengths and makes them so that—'

'Turn that thing off at once,' said Dr Ford, who had entered unnoticed in the middle of Tony's exposition and the continued Brocken performance of the wireless.

'But sir,' said Tony reproachfully, 'I was just telling Mr Knox—'

'Shut up,' said Dr Ford.

Laura altered the knobs so that a talk on beekeeping gently permeated the room.

'But, sir,' pleaded Tony, his blue eyes full of pure scientific research, 'Mr Knox really does need a super het. You see the transformer, Dr Ford, that little box thing on the floor?'

'I'll admit that I see it,' said Dr Ford cautiously, 'but no more.'

'Well, sir, suppose that you took the plug out and put it in here,' said Tony, suiting the action to the word, 'it would—'

There was another crackle, a flash and the light in the wireless set went out.

'Now you've blown a fuse out,' said Dr Ford, with gloomy triumph, 'and thank God, we can't hear any more about bees.'

'Good God! Good God! Is the house on fire?' asked George Knox.

'No, Knox. But the lights are all out,' said Dr Ford, trying the switch by the door. 'You'll have to have a new fuse put in.'

'I'm awfully sorry, sir,' said Tony, 'but I was only explaining the electricity to Mr Knox and somehow the plugs got in the wrong holes. I can easily put a fuse in if you tell me where the main—'

'Sit still and shut up,' said Dr Ford, while Laura confounded herself in excuses for her son. 'What's your present trouble, Knox?'

'Milton,' said the still bewildered George Knox.

On the evening of Easter Tuesday, Laura brought Tony over to Low Rising. George Knox, reposing himself from the fatigues of his day in town, was sitting by the fire in a dressing-gown, with his wife and Dr Ford to keep him company.

'Dear Laura,' said George Knox, 'you will forgive a worn-out and ageing man if he does not rise. That I see you again is indeed ichor, elixir, but take the will for the deed when I tell you that I am almost under orders not to exert myself, am I not, Ford?'

'Not in the least,' said Dr Ford.

'Well, be that as it may,' said George Knox with some annoyance, 'I am glad to see you, Laura, yes, faith, heartily glad. Why should I talk like that?' he added, glaring suspiciously round.

'You can't help it, George,' said Laura, sitting down. 'Now tell me all about the talk.'

'Tell me first,' said George Knox, 'whether you, I will

not say enjoyed, for that is hardly a word to apply to Milton, but whether you found in what I said any one word, any breath, of the integral essence of that great, though domestically unpleasant poet of our notable Commonwealth?'

Tony fixed an inscrutable gaze on his mother, who replied with almost imperceptible hesitation.

'I'm sure it was all perfectly marvellous George, but I want to hear about your part. Were you nervous?'

'Why,' began George Knox, settling himself comfortably, 'why one like myself who, I say it without any mock-modesty, can purge the minds of thousands of readers with pity and contempt, no, contempt is not the word, but let that pass; why, I say, one like myself, master of the written word, should be, by the mere fact of sitting alone, or almost alone, for the presence of the charming youth who was my guide cannot be counted as in any way disturbing, with a manuscript carefully prepared, before him – though manuscript is not the word I should use when my dear wife had so exquisitely, so skilfully, typed it for me with this hand, which I humbly salute,' said George Knox, kissing his wife's hand, 'why it should harrow up my soul and freeze my middle-aged blood, is beyond my power to tell.'

'Tony,' said Dr Ford, seeing that his young friend was preparing to correct this quotation, 'just go and see if my lights are on.'

'But why,' continued George Knox, 'should I harrow *your* blood Laura, blood to which I hesitate to affix an epithet, for though you are not young, nay, Laura, no longer young, you are yet young to me, or is it rather that we grow old together and so do not see the greying, or in my case, the receding hair, the sunken eye, the missing, or in your case, the false, teeth—'

'That's enough, George,' said his wife placidly. 'Laura, dear, do tell us if you liked George's talk.'

'Oh, it's too dreadful,' said Laura, 'but we never heard it. Tony did something with the electricity and everything burst.'

'Mother!' said Tony, who had returned and was standing in the door twisting himself about. 'Mother, I only just plugged in Mr Mallow's set. They oughtn't to make different voltages.'

'I have it! I have it!' cried George Knox, suddenly getting up and striding about.

Everyone looked at him with interest.

'Anne— No, Laura,' said George Knox, 'do you remember this morning, or do I mean last week, when one or perhaps both of you left that door open and I was cudgelling what poor brains I have to remember the allusion that so persistently escaped me?'

'Say "yes",' whispered Anne to Laura.

'Yes, George,' said Laura, trying to make a face at Tony that would make him shut the door.

'*Il faut qu'une porte soit ouverte ou fermée*,' said George Knox with conviction, 'though even that does not – alas! – include the name of the author; which will doubtless return to me when least required, in the bath, at a railway junction, alone on the windy moor; what do I know, but to return to earth; come in at once, my boy, and shut the door, and tell me, without technicalities, for they are as naught to me, or less than naught, though I might as well say more than naught, for how can aught be more than naught, or less if it comes to that— Anne, Anne,' he called to his wife, 'what is it that I want to say?'

'You want to ask Tony what he did to put the wireless out of order,' said Anne calmly. 'What happened, Tony?'

'Well, I didn't do *anything*,' said Tony in an aggrieved tone. 'Mr Mallow lent me his set, and the voltage was a bit different, but it wasn't much, so I plugged it in upstairs in the play-room, because I wanted to hear the electric organ from the Wigan Trocette cinema, and then all the lights went out.'

'I yet fail to grasp the cause and effect,' said George Knox.

'I'll show you, sir,' said Tony, warming to the subject. 'You see, lots of people have different voltages, and you need a transformer if you are going to plug in. It's just the same here, you see, if I took this plug out of your wireless transformer and plugged it in here, all the lights would go out.'

From the black-out which followed three voices emerged.

'Well,' said Dr Ford, as he felt in his pocket for the matches, 'it's a pity we aren't all blind like Milton. He wouldn't have noticed a little thing like this.'

'Your lights *were* out, sir,' said Tony to Dr Ford, 'and I expect the battery's run down.'

'Alfred de Musset!' cried George Knox with the joy of one who has solved a world problem.

First published in Harper's Bazaar, *January 1937*

The Private View

It is true that old Sir Dighton Phelps of Phelps's Galleries knew all about old paintings, and middle-aged Mr Dighton Phelps knew all about modern paintings, and young Mr Dighton Phelps, known as Mr Dighton, knew all about everything, but it was Miss Brown who kept everyone steady. After the rather disastrous season in which the Old Master purchased by Sir Dighton had not ripened into a genuine Mantegna as thoroughly as one would wish, Miss Brown had soothed Mr Phelps and Mr Dighton, and persuaded them that the ripening process was only deferred. In the same unlikely season, Mr Phelps had backed an extremely unsuccessful show by a young man who had roused his temporary and unjustified enthusiasm, and Mr Dighton had managed to offend William Hay, who could make and unmake Mantegnas with a line from his pen. But good Miss Brown had comforted everyone, and though she could not make good the loss in which Mr Phelps's ill-advised investment had landed them, nor conciliate William Hay who was in South America, she was so understanding and so competent and so sympathetic that everyone felt things might have been worse. And now a fresh season had begun, and the Gallery was to open with a memorial loan exhibition of the drawings and paintings of Charles Wilson, an eminent Victorian whose romantic works were a complete drug in the market.

Charles Wilson had been dead for a good many years, but this year, being the centenary of his birth, had seemed to the Phelps family a good peg to hang an exhibition on, especially as they had been quietly buying up Wilsons for some time past. So for several months Sir Dighton and Mr Phelps and young Mr Dighton had been hunting up owners of pictures, and trying to follow changes of ownership through old catalogues, and in fact, short of putting advertisements in *The Times*, which would have roused the suspicion of other dealers, doing all that could be done to get together a representation exhibition. And whichever of them forgot to do a job, or did it badly, or offended an owner, which was easy to do because some picture owners are offended if you do ask for the loan of their pictures and some if you don't, Miss Brown was always at hand to remind, to carry out, to placate. And it was Miss Brown who supplied Amelia Wilson.

'I think, Mr Phelps,' said she to the middle member of the firm, 'it might be useful if we asked Miss Wilson to help us. Charles Wilson was her great-uncle, and she has some of his pictures and would know where others are.'

'How do we get at her?' asked Mr Phelps.

'She is an old friend of mine,' said Miss Brown, 'and I will ask her to lunch and put in a good word.'

Mr Phelps wasn't quite sure if Miss Brown ought to have any acknowledged existence, or any friends outside the galleries, but for the good of the firm he overlooked this individualistic outbreak and not only encouraged the idea, but told Miss Brown to stay as long as she liked at lunch and take it out of petty cash.

So that is why we find Miss Brown and Amelia Wilson having lunch together at Gunter's. A most reckless and unbalanced lunch it was, consisting of brioches and croissants with a great deal of butter, and hot chocolate with a great deal of sugar and cream.

'You see, I'm really on a diet,' said Amelia to Miss Brown, 'but I'm not counting this as one of the days.'

'I'm on a diet too,' said Miss Brown, with much interest. So she and Amelia stuffed themselves with fattening, indigestible, starchy, delicious food, and talked about their strict *régime*, and how they were living entirely on grilled chops with no fat, tomatoes, lettuce, eggs and grapefruit.

'My diet is practically the same as the Hollywood

slimming diet,' said Amelia, 'but of course I don't *dream* of slimming. People are so silly to starve themselves.'

'My diet *is* the Hollywood slimming diet,' said Miss Brown firmly while she ate a large piece of butter with a crumb of brioche sticking to it, 'and I do try to slim.'

As both of these ladies were very nice ordinary-shaped people, neither fat nor thin, it all seemed unnecessary, but evidently gave satisfaction.

'Now, about this exhibition of your uncle's things,' said Miss Brown. 'We can't trace some of his important pictures, and perhaps you will help us. It will be pure kindness on your part, but it may do you good too, because if we get a good boom for Charles Wilsons, you will be able to sell yours if you want to. Only don't sell any, even to our Mr Phelps, without letting me know, because in your case I shall bite the hand that feeds me and see that it doesn't do you down. I suppose you remember your uncle quite well. He must have been an interesting man.'

'I often wish,' said Amelia pensively, 'that my uncle Charles were boiled in a pot, and all his pictures with him. It is quite sickening to go through life as the original of Charles Wilson's *Wide-eyed Innocence*. I don't remember Uncle Charles much except that he had a beard and was rather cross, and I only sat to him once for that picture, and I was six years old and sat very badly and he told Mother for goodness' sake to take the child away, and finished it out of his own head, or from his charwoman's little girl, I forget which. If you were always being introduced as Charles Wilson's niece who sat for *Wide-eyed Innocence*, you'd know what I feel like. It never seems to give one a chance of being oneself, and one is expected to have rather a sacred face about Uncle Charles.'

'But you will help us with the show, won't you? You appear to be Only Surviving Relative, and it will make a good effect.'

Amelia looked at Miss Brown with a shy but hopeful expression.

'I did have an idea,' she said. 'I do dearly love a party, and I thought if it wasn't terribly undignified for a highbrow gallery like yours, we might have a tea-party for the Private View. I could ask all the old friends who knew Uncle Charles, and all the children of old friends who are dead, and all the people who have lent pictures, and if people hear of food they are much more likely to come, and you could have a splendid squash, and it would be a good advertisement. I'd pay for the tea, of course, because I do like a party better than anything in the world, and if the show means that I can sell off Uncle Charles's pictures, I can well afford to gamble on the tea.'

'It's an idea,' said Miss Brown and, paying the bill out of petty cash, which she had taken the precaution to bring with her, she invited Amelia to come round to the gallery then and there, and talk to the directors. Only old Sir Dighton was in, and as he was the most susceptible member of the firm, he agreed at once to let Amelia have her tea-party (though not to pay for it), and took her into his private room to see the Mantegna, which was still ripening.

'How much will you sell it for?' asked Amelia.

Sir Dighton thought of being shocked by her unrefined bluntness, but looking at her agreeable face and figure changed his outlook to fatherly and tolerant amusement.

'It all depends, dear lady, upon the market and, to a lesser degree, upon the favourable or unfavourable verdict of William Hay, who is certainly the ultimate authority on Mantegna, though no more infallible than the rest of us. But probably he is merely a name to you.'

Indeed he was a name to Amelia, but not as Sir Dighton meant it. When two people have met and fallen in love too quickly, and quarrelled too quickly, and separated with hard words which neither of them meant to say, and have both been too proud to write, and one of them has been out of England for three months, the name of each may mean a good deal to the other. Amelia still could not hear William Hay's name without feeling that she was rather drunk in the middle of a display of fireworks. As for William Hay, he still felt that it was all Amelia's fault, but when he read in Buenos Aires, in an old *Times*, that a memorial exhibition of Charles Wilson's works was to be held at Phelps's Gallery, his heart rebelliously hit him in the ribs in an unmistakable way.

So Amelia said, yes, she knew his name.

'We hope he may be in London in time to visit the exhibition of your uncle's works,' said old Sir Dighton. 'Your uncle must have been an interesting man, Miss Wilson.'

Amelia mechanically put on her sacred face and said the right things, and then Sir Dighton left her with Miss Brown.

'If you'll let me have a lot of Private View cards,' said Amelia, 'I'll send them to people with a personal note. And I'd like to compare my list with yours in case we overlap. I have it here all ready made out, because I wanted so much to have a party that I thought I'd be all prepared.'

Miss Brown got out the address book and Amelia crossed out some names on her list and added others. Presently she came to the name of William Hay.

'Do you ask Mr Hay to all your shows?' she enquired.

'Oh yes. He's a tremendous friend of the firm. There was rather a row last year, because our young Mr Dighton had words with him about Signorelli. Very silly of Mr Dighton, who is only a clever amateur,' said Miss Brown, 'but people will get snobbish about pictures. So Mr Hay went off to give good advice in Buenos Aires in a huff, without committing himself about our Mantegna, and we daren't come quite out into the open about it till he comes back, particularly as the Royal British Gallery are jealous, and say it is only a School Of.'

'I hope Mr Hay will come,' said Amelia.

'*Pour cause?*' said Miss Brown, who had rather a good French accent.

'For that very reason,' said Amelia, embarrassed, but determined.

'He will come,' said Miss Brown composedly, and made a note on a pad.

'I'm afraid,' said Amelia, 'I'll have to ask an awful job lot of relations, but they'll not look so bad among the rest, and it will please them frightfully to be remembered, and share in the glory and all. I think I've remembered them all, but I'm bound to leave someone out and give offence, though really with some of the relations, they are so grasping that they'll take offence without your giving it.'

Later in the afternoon, Mr Phelps and Mr Dighton came in from lunch and were told about the plans for the Private View. Both were inclined to be suspicious of the innovation of a tea-party, but Miss Brown flattened all their objections, pointing out that a long table at one end of the large room would not take up much space, and a firm of caterers would arrange everything.

'By the way,' said young Mr Dighton, 'who do you think I saw at lunch?'

As his father and grandfather appeared content to exist in a state of ignorance, good Miss Brown asked who it was.

'Hay,' said young Mr Dighton. 'He's back from Buenos Aires with a very repulsive Dago in tow.'

'Dago?' said Sir Dighton, staring coldly at his grandson.

'Yes, sir. One of those monkey-faced Wops they keep out there. He's rolling, of course, like all of them. Pity it's only a loan exhibition of Wilson's things we're having. He might have bought the lot.'

'What is a pity,' said his grandfather, 'is that you couldn't hold your tongue about Signorelli before Hay went away. We might have done something about the Mantegna if you had been decently civil. Now Hay will probably crab it for all he is worth.'

'That's all right, Grandpapa,' said young Mr Dighton. 'We made it up at lunch and Hay is coming along to see your Genuine Old Master before long. His Dago seemed interested.'

Accordingly young Mr Dighton received a roving commission to catch William Hay, with or without the Dago, give him the best lunch money could buy, and bring him, all nicely oiled as young Mr Dighton vulgarly put it, to see the Mantegna. But London has a great many invitations for a bachelor art critic with a wealthy South American client, and not till the day of the Wilson Private View was Mr Dighton able to secure his victims. After a sumptuous and protracted lunch, William Hay was delivered to old Sir Dighton to discuss the Mantegna, while the Dago, a charming Argentine of simian appearance called García, was handed over to Mr Phelps, who bored him considerably by showing him examples of recent French art.

Meanwhile, young Mr Dighton went in search of Miss Brown, who was talking to a good-looking young woman.

'Let me introduce Mr Dighton Phelps, one of our directors,' said Miss Brown. 'I don't think, Mr Dighton, you have met Miss Wilson whose uncle's pictures we are showing.'

'I am delighted to meet the original Wide-eyed Innocence,' said young Mr Dighton, who prided himself on remembering all about everybody.

'Well, I'm not,' said Amelia nervously, 'at least you wouldn't be if you were me, though that's not exactly what I mean. It is really a curse, and Uncle Charles was always so cross, in spite of his venerable beard. I don't understand about pictures at all, you know.'

'Nor do I,' said young Mr Dighton, with his slightly too ready and too disarming smile. 'We don't pretend to be experts, Miss Wilson, merely salesmen, so you and I can meet on common ground.'

'Well,' said Amelia doubtfully, 'I can't quite believe you. But Uncle Charles didn't like pictures either, except his own. He had a poem about them, which is a very good poem, only it's difficult to get the rhyme exactly right.'

'Oh, do let me hear it,' said young Mr Dighton, with his rather too captivating smile.

Amelia looked at him gravely, and after a pause spoke as follows:

'There's nothing nastier
Than an Old Master.'

For a moment there was silence, till young Mr Dighton could get his ready sense of humour to bear on the poem.

'Perfect, perfect, Miss Wilson,' he cried appreciatively, 'and as you say, most difficult to do justice to. I should like to tell it to Hay. It might encourage him to set proper value on my grandfather's Mantegna.'

'Is Mr Hay in the office still?' asked Miss Brown.

'Yes, he's doing blood tests, or whatever they do,' said young Mr Dighton, with his engaging affectation of ignorance. 'He'll be out soon. I must introduce him to you, Miss Wilson. A delightful creature. Forgive me, I must have a word with my father.'

He darted away, and Amelia looked at Miss Brown.

'It's all right,' said Miss Brown. 'If you want to talk to Mr Hay, I won't let him leave the gallery.'

'I do want to,' said Amelia. 'And it is going to be a very nervous day altogether. You see, Uncle Charles was very forthcoming to his female friends, though all honourable. And two of his very special friends will be here, Lady Buzzard and Mrs Hunt. Lady Buzzard sat to him for several pictures and feels she was his great inspiration. Mrs Hunt never sat to him, but she used to buy his pictures and rather felt she owned him. They aren't very good friends, in spite of their age, which is so great that one might be excused for thinking they were old enough to be sensible.'

'We have had plenty of trouble with them both already,' said Miss Brown. 'They tried to make themselves into a kind of hanging committee, and are both jealous of the other's lendings. You will have to realise, Amelia, that this is their party, not yours.'

'I don't mind a bit. A party is always a party, and anyway Uncle Charles was my uncle, not theirs. Do you think Mr Hay will be long?'

At that moment William Hay was passing through one of the crises which beset art experts. Undoubtedly the Mantegna was a Mantegna – there could be no possible doubt of it. Professor Schramm of Vienna, whose opinion William Hay rated only a little lower than his own, was ready to back him, and if Sir Alured Booth at the Royal British Gallery liked to say it wasn't, that only proved the imbecility of middle fourteenth-century illuminated manuscripts thinking they could plunge into fifteenth-century painting. As far as the genuineness of the Mantegna went, William Hay was prepared to stake his whole professional reputation; but he did not want to do a good turn to the firm of Phelps. In spite of the reconciliation, young Mr Dighton's ill-advised words about Signorelli still rankled, and William Hay did not like to think of the large profit (part of which would ultimately find its way into young Mr Dighton's pocket) which the firm would make if his Argentine client bought the Mantegna. On the other hand, Señor García, who was quite impossibly rich, had come over to England with him expressly to buy Old Masters, and William Hay would be wanting in duty to a client if he didn't let him get in early on the Mantegna. So life became very difficult, and William Hay expressed the greatest admiration to old Sir Dighton and asked if he might come again quietly one day and make up his mind. He then wrung Sir Dighton's hand and walked out of his room into the gallery, and straight into Amelia Wilson.

Both were too much taken aback to remember anything of their quarrel. Their souls were in their names, but before any further word of kindness or explanation could be uttered, Señor García burst out of Mr Phelps's private room, and flung himself upon William Hay, making what were apparently violent protests, in Spanish.

'It is most unfortunate, Hay, that your friend does not speak English,' said Mr Phelps piteously. 'I thought my collection of French triangulists might interest him, but

I was unable to explain their interesting points. Perhaps he would care to look at them later on.'

William Hay conveyed this invitation to Señor García who, looking Mr Phelps firmly in the face, remarked, 'Most horreeble affairs.'

'Perhaps,' said Miss Brown, who wished to give Amelia a chance to speak to her friend, and had never been known to let a client go, 'Señor García speaks French?'

'*Couramment*,' said Señor García with an atrocious accent.

'In that case,' said Miss Brown, in excellent French, 'we might, if *monsieur* desires it, make a little tour of the galleries and regard the pictures of M. Wilsonne, the uncle of mademoiselle,' – García bowed – 'a talent of the most distinguished. A connoisseur such as *monsieur* cannot miss to appreciate the excellence of these pictures, veritable feasts, one can say, of English beauty of before-war.'

Still talking, she led Señor García away to the farther gallery.

'And now, Hay,' said Mr Phelps, 'I want to introduce you to Lady Buzzard, who is most anxious to meet you.'

Lady Buzzard, a tall haggard woman, with smouldering remains of beauty, hung with turquoise chains and crowned with a toque of violets and a floating veil, advanced upon them.

'Dear Lady Buzzard,' said Amelia, automatically assuming her sacred face, 'how very sweet of you to come, and it was so good of you to lend your lovely portrait and the two large pictures.'

'Dear child,' said Lady Buzzard, holding Amelia tightly with one hand to prevent her escape, while with the other she shook hands intensively with William Hay. 'Dear child, you have no idea what anguish it was to me to lend those pictures. Their empty places seem to reproach me from the walls. I do so well remember your dear uncle saying to me, "Give your pictures away, Ida, sell them if you will, but never lend them."'

'Why did he say that?' asked Amelia.

'I will tell you, dear child,' said Lady Buzzard, still holding William and Amelia in a grip of iron in case either of them should get away and talk to any of the other guests who were now pouring into the rooms. 'I will tell you,' she repeated absentmindedly, while her eye roved around in search of other victims. 'You must come to lunch one day and we will have a real talk about your dear, dear uncle and I will show you some of the lovely little sketches I have – things quite unlike his usual work, done only for me. And now, Mr Hay, I want to pin you down to dine with me one day next week and bring your friend Señor García.'

She dropped Amelia's hand and pushed William Hay backwards into a corner so that he could move neither to the right nor the left. Amelia found herself seized by an elderly woman, thin as a skeleton, wound round with striped material and covered from head to foot with a liberal dusting of face powder.

'Dear Mrs Hunt,' said Amelia, 'it was so good of you to come and lend your lovely picture.'

'I am very, very angry with Sir Dighton,' said Mrs Hunt, gripping Amelia's arm with a claw-like hand. 'I offered him three of my Wilsons and he has only taken one. The show is ruined without my *Greta Banks* and my *Blue Eye, Beauty*. Ah, there is William Hay, I must speak to him.'

Releasing Amelia, she intruded her long bony body between Lady Buzzard and William.

'Dear Lady Buzzard, so noble of you to lend all your pictures,' she exclaimed. 'When you only have three, it is positively angelic to part with them, especially when those walls so kill the effect of the paintings. And how delightful to see you back again, Mr Hay. When will you dine?'

But before Hay could answer, Lazy Buzzard interrupted in her masculine voice.

'I was just telling Amelia, dear Mrs Hunt, how lost I feel without my pictures. The empty spaces on the walls seem to reproach me whenever I see them. How I envy you only having been asked for one. One pays the penalty, you know, of having the best of a master's work.'

As Lady Buzzard rearranged her turquoise chains carelessly, to give an air of detachment to her unkind words, William Hay managed to sidle out of his corner with an apology and go across to Amelia.

'I didn't know you would be here,' he said, 'or I wouldn't have come.'

'Why not?'

'You probably don't want me.'

'Oh, William,' said Amelia, whose heart began to break. But before she could express her sentiments, a hand was laid on her arm. She turned round and saw, far below her, a very stout shapeless woman, with grey hair escaping untidily from under a garden hat.

'You don't know me,' said the little woman, with a brave smile.

Amelia smiled bravely back – far more bravely if the truth were known, for William was being snatched from her by old Sir Dighton, and she hadn't the faintest idea who the brave little woman was. By a miracle of guesswork she hazarded an affectionate handgrip, saying, 'Of course I do. It's Popetty.'

'Dear, dear child,' said Popetty, her blue eyes brimming with tears.

'You must forgive me if I call you Popetty,' continued Amelia, all understanding smiles, 'because Uncle Charles always called you that.'

She omitted to add that Uncle Charles invariably

added the epithet hell-cat, and that she had not at the moment the faintest idea of Popetty's surname.

'Dear, dear child,' said Popetty again. 'You know how rarely I come to London, but I had to make this effort, and I shall be able to tell your dear aunt all about this wonderful, wonderful day.'

Now Amelia began to remember. Popetty lived with the widowed sister-in-law of Uncle Charles, but even that didn't supply her with a surname.

'And now, dear child,' said Popetty, 'introduce me to Sir Dighton. We used to meet in old days at Kensal Rise, but he may hardly remember me. I used to paint then, but I fear I have let that talent waste away in a napkin.'

As Popetty wore a large blue enamel cross hanging upon her lumpy form, Amelia felt that it was all somehow very religious. Also she was terribly embarrassed at having to introduce someone whose name she didn't know to Sir Dighton, who was earnestly talking to William. Summoning up her courage, she touched Sir Dighton's elbow.

'Sir Dighton,' she said, without much assurance, 'here is a very old friend who wants to meet you again. I expect you will remember her at Kensal Green.'

Popetty suddenly became very breezy, and laughed in a hearty and alarming way.

'There are still a few years left before we meet at Kensal Green, Sir Dighton,' she said with an obese kind of archness, 'but you haven't forgotten Popetty?'

With one impulse William and Amelia left Sir Dighton to struggle as courteously as possible with his obvious ignorance of Popetty.

'Do you mean,' said William, 'that you don't mind my being here?'

'Mind?' said Amelia, 'Oh, William!'

'Here I am, Amelia dear,' said a cheerful, rather common voice. Starting nervously, Amelia looked round and saw her cousin Olivia, of whom she was slightly ashamed in public.

'It was sweet of you to ask me, dear,' said Cousin Olivia, 'and to send me a card for two. This is your cousin, Freddie. I don't think you've ever met.'

Cousin Freddie, a grey-faced, spare elderly man with a thin moustache, nodded his head morosely.

'He's the dyspeptic one,' said Cousin Olivia. 'His wife has left him, you know, dear,' she continued in a sepulchral voice, 'but perhaps it was for the best. I always say we can't judge others. We're going to have a little tea now, and then a good look at Charles's pictures, quite old familiar faces, and then we shall come back and have another little chat with you, dear.'

She moved briskly off, followed by the deserted Cousin Freddie, but it was too late for Amelia to catch William, who had been again engulfed by Lady Buzzard and forced to give her tea.

Amelia began to despair. There seemed to be no

chance of talking to William without being rude to someone, and Miss Brown had deserted her. The rooms were crowded and the Private View was obviously going to be the success of the season, but it would be no success for Amelia if William went away without an explanation. The rooms were getting hotter and hotter, the roar of grown-up people having tea was getting louder and louder, and Amelia felt her wits deserting her and her throat becoming hoarse and soundless. She fervently wished, not for the first time, that she were one of those courageous pushing women like Lady Buzzard or Mrs Hunt, or even a brave pathetic little woman like Popetty. But if one was a nice ordinary polite woman one couldn't push, and it didn't do any good if one did. Full of bitter thoughts, occasionally catching a glimpse of William's anguished face beyond Lady Buzzard's toque, Amelia stood deserted at her own party, almost crying with fatigue and mortification. With fatal clarity she saw what was about to happen. Cousin Olivia, Cousin Freddie and Popetty were detaching themselves from the crowd and bearing down upon her from different directions. In a moment she would be enveloped and overpowered, and forced in a fit of nervous hospitality to ask them all to lunch the next day. With the courage of despair she opened the nearest door, which happened to be Mr Phelps's office, shut it behind her and, sitting down, burst into silent but bitter tears. At this moment, the Goddess of Boredom, passing in disguise through the galleries, though really there was but little need for disguise where everyone so obviously wore her form and face, saw with her questing eye the approach of three of her disciples, and caused Popetty to drop a bag made of coloured raffia just in front of Cousin Freddie, who gallantly stooped to pick it up.

'Oh, thanks so much,' said Popetty. 'Too careless of me, really,' and she became suitably confused.

'Why,' said Olivia, beaming, 'it's never Popetty.'

'Why, it's Olivia,' cried Popetty. 'Well, of all the coincidences! And this isn't Jack, is it?'

'How *curious* that you should say it is Jack, because we were talking of poor Jack only yesterday, the anniversary of the day on which he passed away. This is Freddie.'

'Of course it is,' said Popetty. 'My dear, this is too wonderful to see you here. Do you remember how Freddie took me for poor Charles's sister-in-law at poor Jack's funeral, and how we all laughed?'

Olivia did indeed remember, and she and Popetty laughed very heartily.

First published in Cornhill Magazine, *November 1934*

Shakespeare Did Not Dine Out

Shakespeare did not dine out. It is a pity, because he could have learned a great deal. By nature, he belonged to the race of guests (as classified by Mr Max Beerbohm) and his sympathies were all on their side. If his friends and patrons had asked him out a little more he would have been the ideal guest, pleased by everything and ready to be amused by anything, and incidentally, he would have picked up several quite useful hints on party-giving. But it was not to be. I do not know if history has any light to throw on the subject, but every jot of internal evidence in the plays supports the statement: Shakespeare did not dine out.

Take, for example, the party given by Old Capulet. One must allow that it was largely his own fault that the evening was not a success. To begin with, he sent out invitations for at least twenty-five people by a servant who could not read the addresses. By pure luck the letters reached their destinations, but it seems that no hour was named, for when the guests arrived the hostess and her daughter were not down and the servants, who lost their heads on the slightest provocation, set the party down to supper and spend the rest of the evening getting in each other's way. The course of the evening is a little obscure, but the Capulets must at length have joined their guests at the table, for after some unseemly skirmishing among various servants who would never have been allowed further than the scullery in any well-run establishment, the whole company got as far as the hall, where Old Capulet made jokes in very questionable taste to set things going. After this, the party went fairly well, as a dance is always arranged to fill out the scene, but the guests were disheartened and when the slight excitement of a row between two young men had subsided, they said that they must go. It appears that one went to Capulet's house prepared to accept anything, or else Romeo, who is usually the only one in fancy dress, would have attracted more notice. But the suppers must have had a rather sinister reputation. The host only had to announce more refreshments for the guests to leave in a body.

This one would think enough to damp a host; but no: the devoted Capulet only a few days later decided to give another party, and as everyone was in mourning he thought it suitable to make all the preparations at night. (Why the servants ever stayed in that house is a mystery.

Or perhaps they didn't, as it may be noted that one of them didn't know who his master's daughter was when questioned by a guest.) From sunset till three in the morning was spent baking and making pastry, with perpetual interference from the master of the house, while Lady Capulet, otherwise a woman of some character, gave up any attempt to control the household and contented herself with a few acid words to her husband about leaving the maids alone.

And that is supposed to be the normal way of entertaining among aristocratic families. Are we to conclude from this that Southampton and Essex did their own housekeeping and made such a fiasco of their parties that the guests left? Rather let us deduce that Shakespeare did not dine out and had very little notion of how parties are organised. No self-respecting host would allow his servants to get the upper hand so completely as Shakespeare does.

Again, what is the percentage of parties in good society which are broken up by the arrival of an uninvited ghost? Or how often are private theatricals interrupted by the host starting up with a loud groan and leaving the room?

The good breeding of the guests is, in these cases, markedly superior to that of the hosts. When the late Banquo came to Macbeth's dinner-party and would disappear and reappear like the Cheshire cat, none of the guests turned a hair, but continued to drink wine from pasteboard. It would have been disconcerting to any ordinary guests, because, as a rule, the lights go out (with the exception of two torches carried by male impersonators in kilts) and a great ray from above lights on Banquo; or in more ambitious productions a transparency in the dining-room wall is illuminated. But these guests were of different metal: unshaken by the peculiar remarks of their host and the obvious ill-temper of their hostess, they continued their Barmecide feat till the hostess turned them out, when, still unmoved, they retired with a Scoto-Roman salute.

The same Japanese stoicism is found in the guests at King Claudius' party. They cannot have had a comfortable evening because they always sit on a long bench slanting away from the stage with their backs half turned to the players. The King and Queen have their throne in an equally uncomfortable position, and really could not have seen much of the play without wringing their own necks. The only person whose seat commands a good view is Hamlet, only he will lie on the floor, which is such a truly wretched position to see anything acted on a platform. And when the audience do try to hear the play, Hamlet will talk all the time. One feels it a great pity that Cressida could not have been at the party, as he would have then met his match in back-chat. But for the patient guests it is enough to be at a party at all, and they enjoy every moment of it until the King, revolted by this Grand

Guignol rubbish, has all the lights turned up and rushes out of the room. Then only do the guests get up and go with a Dano-Roman salute.

Now, can we suppose that any of Shakespeare's patrons would have given such outrageously improbable parties? No! Shakespeare was not invited to good parties, and knew nothing of the duties of a host. In fact he disliked hosts. He despised them. Remember Timon's second dinner-party. It cannot be called good form to give your guests plates of warm water and then throw it in their faces – though doubtless great fun. Timon had lived far beyond his income, assisted by a most incompetent butler who confesses that his only effort to check the household expenditure was to retire him to a wasteful cock and set his eyes at flow. Did Timon try to retrench? He only tried to borrow large sums of money at five minutes' notice and then, in spite at his failure, maltreated his guests. But the good guests remained almost unmoved. Not until he threw the dishes at them in a final transport of rage would they leave the table, and almost immediately they were back again, but uttering no unmanly complaints. One of them did indeed bemoan the loss of his cap, but it was quickly found again, and when one reflects how attached elderly foreigners are to their little black skull-caps, one does not blame him.

Only once does Shakespeare betray any real sympathy with the difficulties of a host. All hosts – and most guests – know how impossible it is to remember one's friends' names, not to mention their faces. Poor King Claudius, harassed by an intermittently buried brother, a well-meaning but stupid wife, a really trying nephew, and guns going off every time he drank, could not remember faces. Two courtiers had audience of him, young men of fashion much alike in type, and when he had asked them to look after Hamlet he dismissed them with the words—

'Thanks, Rosencrantz and gentle Guildenstern.'

Of course, he had given the wrong names to the wrong owners, but they would not have minded. It is something to have one's name remembered by a king even if he gives it to someone else. But the queen, so kind and so wanting in tact, had to correct him with a marked emphasis:

'Thanks, *Guildenstern* and gentle *Rosencrantz*.'

Of course, they were equally delighted that the queen should remember their real names; but it was very uncomfortable for Claudius.

If any further proof is needed of Shakespeare's unfortunate ignorance of the customs of decent society, one need only turn to the dinner-party in *Cymbeline*, perhaps one of the most embarrassing of the many manqué parties in the plays.

A Roman gentleman, Philario, invited a few friends to

dine: a Frenchman, a Dutchman, a Spaniard and another Roman. The fifth guest, an Englishman called Posthumus, was late, and to pass the time the company discussed him rather disparagingly. Philario, who had lost control of his party at an early stage, was very uncomfortable about it, especially as Posthumus was just arriving and likely to overhear the conversation. So he said, 'Here he comes,' in a loud whisper, and in came Posthumus rather showily dressed in a sort of kilt with his shirt very low in the neck, red hair, and a large solitaire diamond. I cannot think why Philario invited five people, each speaking a different language, on the same evening. He may have been a Rotarian and hoped that getting together would promote international friendship, but if so he was doomed to failure. In the first place, the Dutchman and the Spaniard never once opened their mouths in the course of the evening and must have had a wretchedly dull time, forgotten by their author and ignored by the rest of the party. Posthumus and the Frenchman did enter into conversation, but their language is so peculiar that one is forced to conclude they were both speaking Italian out of compliment to their host and neither of them speaking it very well. As for the host, it was in vain that he invited his party to recline in a Roman manner at his ill-spread board. He and the Frenchman were immediately elbowed out of the conversation, while Posthumus and Iachimo, the Roman guest, got up an argument respecting Posthumus' wife and whether she was likely to be any better than she should be. Philario tried to stop them and was ignored. They made a bet on the matter, and Philario with more goodwill than elegance said he would have it no lay, but his guests talked him down and left the supper together without so much as draining an empty goblet and all the table laid for nothing.

While it is true that I have no means (short of hiding in the clock-case) of knowing how gentlemen do talk at men's dinner-parties, I imagine that their ordinary talk is more seemly though probably quite as dull.

The only excuse that can be made for these unsuccessful parties is that they are all given by foreigners. And foreigners are peculiar and un-English and perhaps on the whole it does them credit that their parties should be peculiar and un-English too. But at the Boar's Head, or at Justice Shallow's house in Gloucestershire, they knew how to enjoy themselves. A depressing doubt creeps in that we might not have enjoyed ourselves as much as they did. We might have felt rather priggish and out of place and been inclined to put down Falstaff and Shallow – those chosen companions of our refined minds – as coarse and boring; in which, indeed, we should have been perfectly right. But there is no doubt that they were extremely competent at running their own parties.

It is not till we reach the last of the historical plays that we find another party at which host and guests enjoyed themselves equally: Wolsey's entertainment for Henry

VIII. Of course, Mr Edward German's delightful music was a great help, and a feeling of security was given by the presence of the old original guests whom we find seated at long tables, only too pleased to be invited and thoroughly appreciating the conversation of the smart set. There was no trouble with the servants; a large party came on in fancy dress and gave a most creditable dancing display; and finally an excellent hot supper was served. I think this must be a reminiscence of the one really good party to which Shakespeare was invited. But perhaps, shrewd reader, you will remark that Beaumont or Fletcher wrote that scene. To this I will merely reply with a verse of the Swan of Avon which is doubtless familiar to you:

'Tut, that's a foolish observation.'

First published in Cornhill Magazine, *August 1928*

The Great Art of Riding

One afternoon at the beginning of the summer holidays, Mrs Morland was writing in the drawing-room of her house at High Rising. Her youngest son Tony was engaged in making model battleships out of pieces of firewood in a corner of the room, talking aloud to himself as he did so. Laura Morland by long practice could dissociate herself entirely from her son's flow of talk, and while he recited aloud page after page of Jane's *Fighting Ships*, she was able to grapple with her latest serial story of Madame Koska. She had just, to her own great satisfaction, invented a new kind of villain who under the disguise of a traveller in silk was trying to introduce violently flammable material into the best dressmaking houses, so that Westminster Abbey and everyone in it should be burnt to cinders on the occasion of a Royal wedding, when she became conscious of a more than usually urgent note in her son's voice.

She looked up, pushing her hair back with her pencil, and stared at Tony as at some entirely unfamiliar object.

'Mother,' said Tony, 'would you paint the *Adrian* black or grey?'

'Paint Adrian?' asked Laura, still in the trance-like state to which literary composition always reduced her, and wondering why her publisher, Adrian Coates, should be painted at all.

'Mother,' said Tony reproachfully, 'I thought you *knew* my new cruiser was called the *Adrian*. It belongs to the A class, Mother. Look, Mother, there is the *Adrian* after Mr Coates, and the *Anne* after Mrs Knox, and the *Annie* after Annie at Low Rising, and the *Amy* after Mrs Birkett, and the *Anabasis* because of Xenophon, and the *Armadillo*. Don't you think *Armadillo* is a good name, Mother? Mother, look at them.'

Hypnotised as always by her son's courteous persistence, Laura got up and went over to Tony's corner. On the floor were five little ships, exquisitely carved, and guns no thicker than a needle. How Tony made them with a blunt pocket-knife was his own secret. The sixth ship, the *Adrian*, he held up for his mother's inspection.

Laura, who had not craftsman's hands, was deeply impressed by these enchanting models, and was about to say something in their praise when her son saved her the trouble.

'Mother, isn't the *Adrian* splendid?' he said earnestly.

'Isn't she just like a real ship? Mother, I bet if you were small enough the *Adrian* would look like the *Hood*. Do you think I ought to paint her black or grey, Mother?'

'I don't know,' said Laura feebly, adding mentally, 'and I don't care.'

'Oh Mother, you must know. Would you like black?'

'Black would be very nice.'

'But, Mother, warships aren't really black, they are grey. Mother, shall I paint the *Adrian* grey? Dr Ford,' he pursued, addressing their old friend who came in at that moment, 'would you paint the *Adrian* black or grey? Of course, black is the wrong colour, but I've got some black enamel paint. Or should I get some grey and paint her grey? She would look splendid in grey and—'

'Shut up,' said Dr Ford. 'I want to talk to your mother.'

Tony subsided into mutterings about people who didn't understand about warships, while Dr Ford continued to Laura, 'I want your help, Mrs Morland. There's a very decent little chap I know, used to be a groom at Rising Castle, who has had a rough spin. His wife is ill and there are two children and they are in difficulties. Lord Stoke has lent him a horse, and Knox has lent him the money to buy a pony and he wants to give lessons to children. Mrs Gould is going to let Rose and Dora ride. He's very cheap. Would you let Tony join?'

'Oh Mother,' interrupted Tony, looking up from the *Adrian*, 'can I? I have ridden at Lord Stoke's. I have a kind of gift for riding and horses, so that I can't fall off. Oh Mother, can I?'

'I suppose I'll have to say yes,' said Laura to Dr Ford, 'though if you had any tact you wouldn't have asked me in front of Tony. This will be far worse than bicycling. It isn't only being thrown off and killed,' she said in an abstracted voice, her eyes fixed on a vision of misfortunes to come, 'but having his face kicked in by the horse's hoofs, or being dragged for miles by a stirrup, or being rolled on and spending the rest of his life on a stretcher, besides ordinary falls and broken collar-bones.'

But Laura's objections were overridden by Dr Ford's anxiety to help his protégé and Tony's wish to show off as a rider for the benefit of Rose and Dora, so a plan was made to meet at the Vicarage next morning.

No sooner had Dr Ford gone than Tony dashed upstairs leaving his fleet strewn about the floor, so that it was not Stoker's fault when, coming in later with the tea-tray, she walked on the *Adrian*, crushing her to a shapeless wreck.

'Oh Stoker,' cried Laura, 'you've trodden on Tony's ship. What will he do?'

'Won't know nothing about it if you don't go telling him,' said Stoker, and bending with some difficulty she picked up the wreck and put it behind a box on the mantelpiece.

'Out of sight out of mind as the saying is,' she remarked, 'and I'd be out of *my* mind if I was to worry about Master Tony's fancies. Did you wish him to put them corduroys of his on for tea and Mrs Gould and the young ladies coming?'

'No, I didn't,' said Laura, as Tony came into the room with a swaggering air. He was wearing his school football jersey, the corduroy breeches, khaki scout's stockings and black shoes. Round his neck was a muffler, his hair was all on end, and he carried his best leather gloves with an air of abandon.

'Go and take off those disreputable things at once, Tony,' said his mother.

'Oh, but Mother, if I'm going to ride tomorrow I must get used to my breeches. Breeches are quite different from knickerbockers, Mother. You have to sit quite differently.'

In proof of which Tony sat down astride, facing the back of his chair, and looked at his mother with an expressionless stare. As Mrs Gould and the girls now arrived, Laura could not let loose her annoyance on Tony, who behaved like an angel during tea, not even boasting when the next day's ride was discussed. He then volunteered to see the Gould family home and by supper-time had changed back into ordinary clothes. Laura, immersed again in her villain, forgot all about Tony's misdeeds, which was exactly what he had hoped.

Next morning, Tony, now strongly entrenched in his peculiar riding dress, arrived alone at the Vicarage. Laura sent the excuse of work, but as a matter of fact she had determined not to see her son thrown, kicked, dragged or mangled, preferring to imagine all these things by herself. Rose and Dora, very neat in jerseys and jodhpurs, were standing at the gate, while a little man in leggings led a small horse and a rough-coated pony up and down the lane.

'That's a decent horse,' said Tony, pulling on his gloves in a devil-may-care way.

'She's a mare,' said Dora. 'Her name is Amber.'

Tony's face became blank.

'So is the pony,' added Dora, driving her victory home.

'Ponies aren't mares, they are just ponies,' said Tony coldly.

'All right,' said Dora, 'cats are dogs.'

'Hush, Dora,' said Mrs Gould. 'Now, which of you is going to ride? Jenkins, which will you take first?'

'The young ladies, mum,' said the groom, touching his cap. 'I can see this young gentleman is new to it, and the pony won't be so fresh when the young ladies have been on her.'

Tony's face of chilly contempt passed unnoticed as Jenkins led the horses down the lane to the big Vicarage paddock where the gardener had put up a rough jump about three feet high.

'You young ladies can both ride,' said Jenkins.

In a moment Rose was on the horse and Dora on the pony. Both little girls had ridden a good deal, owing to the kindness of Lord Stoke and other neighbours. Rose, usually timid and awkward, was another creature on horseback, entirely sure of herself, while Dora, with less style, was equally at home. Rose leading, the little girls trotted and cantered about the large field while Tony looked on, a sense of injustice swelling in his bosom. In all their games he had been the leader, humbly admired by his young friends; now they were suddenly exalted above him, belonging to the enviable world of horsemen. It was hard after he had dressed so dashingly for the part and boasted to Stoker quite unbearably the night before of what he was going to do, to find himself neglected and left out as a mere beginner. For the first time in his life he felt a pang of envy for Rose and Dora's superior gifts, and a hard lump came into his throat, a lump which uncomfortably dissolved and rose in him, giving him a pricking feeling in his nose and making his eyes look a little pink.

'It's all right, sir,' said Jenkins, mistaking Tony's emotion, 'the pony's as quiet as a lamb.'

Tony turned away and now luckily Rose came past at full tilt, and under cover of the noise of her horse's hoofs, Tony was able to sniff loudly and satisfyingly, so that there was no need for him to use the spotted silk handkerchief which he had so proudly put into his breeches pocket that morning. After Rose had taken the jump several times in professional style, and Dora had bucketed over with her pony in a useful but inelegant way, the groom told them to dismount.

'Better take those gloves off, sir,' he said, as Rose and Dora led their horses up to the gate near which Tony was standing. 'You'll need your hands to hold the reins.'

At this witticism, Dora guffawed loudly. Tony darted a baleful glance at her by which she was entirely unimpressed. Rose, feeling Tony's discomfort, offered to take care of the gloves for him and drew Dora away.

'Other side, sir,' said Jenkins as Tony approached the pony on the off side.

'I know,' said Tony. 'As a matter of fact, lots of people do get up on the right-hand side.'

'Lots get down that way too,' said Jenkins, but as Dora was not within earshot and Tony, one foot in the stirrup, his right leg clawing madly in the air in his efforts to get it over the pony's back, did not hear him, the joke fell flat.

'Haven't ridden much before, have you, sir?' asked Jenkins kindly as he arranged the stirrups.

'Several times,' said Tony. 'I'm pretty good with horses, I went to the point to point races with Mrs Knox and I picked most of the winners. I don't know how it is, but I seem to know about horses—'

'Keep your elbows down, sir,' said Jenkins, getting on to the mare.

'—and they have an instinct for people that like them,'

continued Tony, riding uneasily to the pony's short trot. 'I bet this pony knows I'm—a—friend—of—horses.'

The last words were jerked out of him, and he bit his tongue with such violence that his conversation was temporarily stemmed. When he and Jenkins got round the field again, they found an addition to the audience in the shape of George Knox, the biographer, and his wife, who were leaning over the gate talking to Rose and Dora.

'Hullo, Mr Knox, hullo, Mrs Knox,' cried Tony, 'do you see me on the pony? I rode it all round the field at a trot. Some people don't like trotting, but I do. I bet I could trot for about twenty miles, easily. Look at me, Mr Knox.'

Intoxicated by an audience and the delightful smell of horses and leather, Tony uttered a loud shriek. The pony gave a start and plunged away across the field, carrying Tony, elbows in the air and feet well out, along with it in its course.

'Oughtn't you to go after him, Jenkins?' asked Anne Knox anxiously. 'He might fall off.'

'I know his sort soon as I set eyes on the young gentleman,' he said. 'A young gentleman like that one never comes to no harm. He'll never learn to ride, not if he was to ride all his life, but he'll stick to the horse somehow.'

And sure enough, as he spoke, the pony turned round and came back with its jubilant rider.

'Mr Knox,' shouted Tony as soon as he was within hearing, 'did you see me?'

'Good God, boy,' said George Knox, 'who in possession of the sense of sight could help seeing you? Who that has seen you could forget? Mazeppa on the Margate sands. I trust I make myself clear,' he said courteously to Jenkins.

'Yes, sir,' said the groom, who was accustomed to gentlemen and therefore unmoved by George Knox's comparison.

'Or Leech's Mr Briggs,' continued George Knox, 'which perhaps makes my meaning more patent.'

'You couldn't exactly have a patent *meaning*, sir,' said Tony pityingly. 'You could have a patent *invention*. Unless of course it was something you said that other people didn't understand unless they knew what it meant. There's a chap at school who always says "Tunk" when you speak to him. It's awfully funny, don't you think, sir – Tunk? You could call Tunk a patent meaning,' he continued, encouraged by the little girls' giggles, 'because it's his own patent idea. If another chap says Tunk, he gets in an awful rage. Did you see me go off at full speed, Mrs Knox?'

'Tunk?' said George Knox. 'Tunk? Anne, have I taken leave of my senses, or has that boy? What the devil does he mean by Tunk?'

'It's what the chap says at school,' said Tony, speaking to every point of the compass as the pony fidgeted round in a circle. 'He says Tunk whenever anyone speaks to him. One day Mr Prothero spoke to him, and he said Tunk, and Mr Prothero—'

But Jenkins, who had borne with gentlefolk as long as he could, now interrupted to ask Tony if he would like to jump.

'Does the pony like jumping?' asked Tony rather anxiously.

'That's all right, sir. Nothing to be afraid of,' was the groom's unfeeling answer. 'Take her at it easy, sir, and keep forward when she goes over and you'll be all right.'

'Go on, Tony,' shrieked Rose and Dora.

'Give me your whip, then,' said Tony to Rose.

'Wait till we see how you can jump, sir, and then we'll see about a whip,' said Jenkins. 'Now, grip her with your knees and take her over.'

The pony, a hardened animal, wearily tolerant of children, was kind enough to trot Tony up to the jump and take him over it. Yards of sky appeared between Tony and the saddle, but as Jenkins had predicted, nothing could permanently dislodge him. Slipping from side to side, stirrups flying, the luck of cheerful riders was with him, and he came trotting back to his friends.

'Forewarned is forearmed,' said George Knox in a loud voice as Tony approached with flapping elbows and a joyful pink face, 'and I will in no wise consent to listen to what you are infallibly going to say, my boy, and indeed I propose to forestall you. I did see you approach the jump; I did see you rise like the phoenix from the saddle, perhaps an unjustifiable metaphor, for between a saddle and a funeral pyre the relationship is obscure, yet let it pass; I did see you, Gilpin-wise clinging to neck and mane till equilibrium resumed her sway; I do at this very moment see you returned, and will not admit, though hell itself should gape – and why, by the way, Anne, do our tragedians pronounce that word when occurring in the immortal tragedy of *Hamlet* as Garp? Do we see some analogy with the custom by which the clergy allude when in the sacred edifice, though never, so far as my recollection and experience serve me, outside it, to the common ancestor of the Jewish race as Arbraham? – I will not, I say, admit that you showed any spark of horsemanship, of the *manège*, of the *haute école*.'

'I say, sir,' said Tony, who had been waiting with deference for George Knox to finish whatever it was that he was saying, 'did you see me take the jump? Did you see me go over, sir? I have a sympathy for ponies and I knew exactly—'

'Good God, good God,' shouted George Knox, 'am I then a thing of naught, unheard, unhonoured?'

'Tunk,' said Dora, very impertinently, upon which all three children had wild giggles and Anne Knox, trying not to laugh, did her best to pacify her husband.

'You can try the mare, sir,' said Jenkins. 'She's an easier jumper than the pony.'

'I'm much better on a real horse,' said Tony, alighting heavily from the pony and valiantly tackling the mare.

'Some people might think a horse more dangerous than a pony, but if you have an instinct for horses you are all right. Ponies are only for kids,' he added, looking witheringly at Dora.

'Tunk,' said Dora.

Tony gave his bridle rein a shake and cantered scornfully away. At this moment, Laura, who had found work quite impossible owing to the visions of a mangled and dying son which had obtruded themselves upon her mind, came down the lane. She was just in time to see Tony heading for the jump.

'Is he all right, George?' she asked anxiously. 'Will he fall off, ought I to stop him, is it safe?'

'Yes, no, no, yes,' was George Knox's answer.

'What do you mean, George, by Yes, No?'

'I was merely, my dear Laura, answering your unnecessary questions categorically. Tony is all right, he will not fall off, you ought not to stop him, it is—'

'He has jumped it!' Laura cried in a loud peacock scream, and then began to cry.

'Cheer up, Laura,' said Anne Knox. 'Tony is perfectly safe.'

It's all right, mum,' said Jenkins, used to mothers. 'The young gentleman will never make a rider, not what you'd call a rider, but he's got plenty of pluck.'

On hearing this, Laura cheered up, and wiping her eyes was ready to greet her returning son.

'Mother,' said he in an offhand way, 'she's a decent little mare. She's just about up to my weight. Mother, I shall call my new ship *Amber* instead of *Adrian*. The mare is Amber. *Amber*, Mother, after the mare. It's a jolly good name, *Amber*.'

'Oh Tony, I'm terribly sorry,' said Laura, 'but you left your ships about on the floor and Stoker trod on the *Adrian*.'

Amber, impatient for the end of the lesson which she knew had to be nearly over, gave her head a jerk, pulled the reins from Tony's hands, and began to crop the grass. Tony, overcome with surprise, fell lumpishly off and rolled on the ground.

'What did I tell you, sir?' said Jenkins, picking up Amber's reins. 'Grip her with your knees.'

'A person can't grip with corduroy breeches,' said Tony, getting up. 'If I had proper riding trousers I could stick on any horse. The *Adrian* is a rotten ship anyhow, Mother, because I painted her black and battleships ought to be grey. Come on, Rose and Dora.'

While the grown-ups followed the three children back up the lane Tony could be heard laying down, from his deep experience, the rules of horsemanship to his friends. As they parted at the Vicarage gate, he pulled his mother's arm.

'Mother,' he said, 'can Rose and Dora come to tea this afternoon? They would like to see my ships. I shall make a new ship this afternoon and call it the *Amber*. Rose and Dora don't know about battleships, so I thought it would be useful for them to learn. Can they come, Mother?'

'Certainly,' said Laura.

'Tunk,' said Dora.

'That's absolute rubbish,' said Tony. 'If you had any sense you'd know that Tunk has a patent meaning that *you* can't possibly understand.'

And he walked away after his mother with the bow-legged gait that a lifetime spent among horses alone imparts.

First published in Harper's Bazaar, *September 1935*

A Nice Day in Town

'Hot water bottle if I can, elastic if they've got any, sponge-bag for Tony, umbrella re-covered, chocolate though it's pretty hopeless, theatre tickets, brandy if any,' said Mrs Morland, the well-known novelist, checking a list she had brought into the kitchen. 'Anything else, Stoker?'

Mrs Morland's almost too faithful maid, whose good-humoured bulk had not been in the least decreased by the rationing of food, looked with kindly contempt at her mistress.

'We could do with a pair of kippers,' she said, 'if you was to see any, and the bottom's right out of the saucepan I do the chicken's food in, but saucepans is something you'll *not* get. Still, there's no harm in trying as they say, and anyway you'll have a nice day in town. Do you good to have a change. Which train are you going by?'

'The 9.22, I suppose?' said Mrs Morland. 'I wish I could take the car, but it would be unpatriotic, besides not having the petrol. I suppose if one really wanted to help the Government one wouldn't use one's petrol ration at all.'

'Silly, that'd be,' said Stoker. 'Same as when you gave the aluminium saucepans to the Government, and all the Government ever saw of them was the Council Lorry came from Southbridge to collect them off the dump and Mr Brown at the garage says he was over at Southbridge on business the next day and happening to pass the remark in the Red Lion that there must have been enough saucepans to make a dozen aeroplanes the young lady at the Red Lion said she knew for a fack that the Council drivers was all giving aluminium saucepans to their wives.'

'So I'll have breakfast at eight, Stoker,' said Mrs Morland coldly, for in common with thousands of other housewives she had long and bitterly repented the impulse that had made her sacrifice three saucepans, a colander and a three-tiered steamer to her country, and had vowed never to give anything again except under compulsion.

Before going to bed that night she rang up her old friend Anne Knox, who had been her secretary before she married the celebrated author George Knox, just to have a gossip, and was justly rewarded for using the telephone unnecessarily, for Mrs Knox with many apologies asked her if she could find time to go to the family house in Rutland Gate and find a French book of which her husband was in urgent need for his life of Henri IV, a task for which, being as he often remarked Catholic by birth, Presbyterian by marriage, and nothing by conviction, he felt himself to be eminently fitted.

'Oh, blast!' said Mrs Morland as she hung up the receiver. 'That means at least half an hour wasted.'

Next morning, armed with a large shopping basket containing paper for wrapping the problematic fish, a string bag for any overflow, a light rug, her gas mask slung across one shoulder and her bag with a long strap across the other, Mrs Morland drove down to the station and parked her car. As she stood in the queue at the Booking Office her attention was caught by an announcement pasted rather askew on the wall, bearing the legend in red lettering IS YOUR JOURNEY REALLY NECESSARY?

'Yes, *and* no,' said Mrs Morland thoughtfully aloud to herself, to the great terror of Rear Admiral Jones R.N. (Retd), who looked upon women who wrote books as a landsman might look upon a mermaid, with attraction and some fear. 'I mean of course I needn't go *anywhere*, but if one is to go anywhere at all one must go somewhere, and I can't go to London and get the book George Knox wants unless I *do* go to London. Day return, please,' she added to the booking clerk, and when the usual rather addled conversation as to whether a day ticket would entitle her to come back on the 4.10 or not, even if it had been changed to the 4.00, had taken place, she walked to the far platform, hoping in common with the whole shopping population of High Rising to find a partly empty carriage, choosing, as was her custom, a non-smoking compartment.

The train was bitterly cold and she was glad to wrap her rug round her knees. At the next station a very unattractive couple got in and took out cigarette cartons. Mrs Morland shrieked inwardly. She did not see any reason why people should disobey railway regulations, she knew pretty well the reception she would get if she drew their attention to the non-smoking notice; and it was just possible that they were not really going to smoke. But this supposition was ill-founded. The woman, who was dressed in sham ocelot, with ladders on the fronts of her stocking, and had dark greasy ringlets confined by a dirty blue fillet, lit her cigarette and then her companion's.

'I am so sorry,' said Mrs Morland, with great courage and disliking the sound of her own voice so much that she felt for the moment quite sympathetic towards the smokers, 'but this is a non-smoking carriage.'

The couple looked at her.

'Ow,' said the woman. 'I thought they smoked everywhere now.'

'It isn't my fault,' said Mrs Morland, becoming more and more apologetic and despising herself more and more for so becoming. 'It's just the regulations.'

'Djer mind if I smoke?' said the man.

This was awful, putting Mrs Morland as it did hopelessly into the position of an aristocratic oppressor of The People, but having gone so far she stuck to her guns and said, 'I *am* so sorry, but I did get into this carriage specially because I don't like smoke. There are heaps of smokers along the corridor.'

The man ground out his cigarette on the seat of the carriage, while the woman laid hers, still alight, on the ledge of the window and began to make up her very dirty face. Her companion took out a penknife and devoted himself to cleaning his nails, carrying on a mumbled conversation the burden of which appeared to be the doings and probable future fate of 'Some People', so that what with this, and what with the sickening smell of the cigarette that lay burning itself out, Mrs Morland almost wished that she had not spoken. But not quite, for although the rest of the travellers had afforded her no support and indeed dissociated themselves from her by silence and a hermit-like retirement behind their newspapers, she knew that they were secretly grateful.

Arrived in London, Mrs Morland forced her way into a bus which put her down near the large store with which she usually dealt. Having, after a sickening moment of despair, found her shopping list, she went towards the Wines and Spirits. Here, trying not to think about the depressing notice which said *No more orders for sherry can be taken*, she took her place in the queue of hopeful shoppers. Since her last visit to London, the department had been considerably changed. Instead of the familiar counter where she had been accustomed to place her modest orders were two tables where girls were efficiently and uninterestedly taking the names of customers who had registered and informing the rest that it was no use waiting. When Mrs Morland got to the desk she was informed that her name would come up in rotation for a bottle of brandy in ten days or a fortnight. A chauffeur and a clergyman then made a massed attack on the desk and Mrs Morland was pushed into the arms of a little wizened assistant with whom she had often dealt.

'Good morning, Mr Siskin,' she said. 'It all seems rather a mess, doesn't it?'

'Sad days these, indeed, madam,' said Mr Siskin, his eyes brimming. 'When I think of the shipments we used to get, and now having to ration the customers that have looked to us for so many years, it makes me realise what we are Up Against. It fair breaks my heart, madam, to see ladies like you standing in a queue instead of "Good day, Mr Siskin, twelve dozen of the usual and a dozen three star whiskies and a half of the usual brandy, or six dozen of the usual Burgundy and a case of Bollinger '23". Still, so long as we win I suppose it's all right. Good morning, madam.'

Mrs Morland, flattered by Mr Siskin's rehearsal of orders such as she had never dreamed of giving, nor could have afforded, thanked him and made her way to the perfumery department where many empty glass cases bore silent witness to the dearth of powder, scents, nail-paint, lip-stick and other necessities.

'I suppose,' said Mrs Morland apologetically to a young lady when she had finished talking to another young lady, 'you haven't a hot water bottle.'

'We've got some nice hot-bottle covers, modom, in pink plushette,' said the young lady, examining her nails which would have reflected credit upon a Mandarin of the First Class.

'I mean a bottle. A rubber one,' said Mrs Morland.

'Oh, *that!* You won't get that anywhere, modom, the Government won't allow it,' said the young lady and resumed her conversation.

Mrs Morland, depressed, enquired about a sponge-bag, to which the young lady with infinite condescension replied, 'Sold out, modom, and no more expected,' and, to avoid further persecution by customers, went away to her lunch. So Mrs Morland took the lift down to the ironmongery.

Here the scene was even more desolate. Where once fish-kettles had hung like bunches of grapes from the ceiling, saucepans had been piled to tottering heights, kettles had stood on shelves in serried rows, whole *batteries de cuisine* had been grouped with tender art about a pyramid of baking tins, all was now silence and gloom. Gone were the piles of zinc pails that impeded progress at the corner where fire-irons looked like a giant game of spillikins. Upon the counter formerly laden with tin-openers, tea-strainers, iron-stands, egg-whisks, perforated ladles, and all the small fry of the kitchen, stood a personal weighing-machine and a blue and white enamel pie-dish; behind the counter, Mr Hobson, once autocrat of some dozen assistants, drooped disconsolate.

Mrs Morland, feeling rather as if she were brawling in church, murmured an enquiry about saucepans.

'We did have a dozen last week, madam,' said Mr Hobson, 'but it was in and out. The ladies were down on them in a moment. But I have a nice enamel pie-dish, really a nice handy thing in the kitchen, only twenty-seven and sixpence.'

Mrs Morland said apologetically that she was really looking for a saucepan; or a kettle perhaps. 'Or we still have this personal weighing-machine,' said Mr Hobson. 'Very nice for the bathroom, though I believe the spring's broken. No, madam, no chance of saucepans or kettles till our next quota and I don't know when that will be nor if they'll send us anything. We just have to take what we can in these days. Still, the great thing is to keep going, I always say.'

Mrs Morland refused the pie-dish or the weighing-machine, said a few words of cold comfort to Mr Hobson and went away, feeling guilty.

After this depressing interview she was much cheered to find a sudden glut of chocolate in the otherwise Sahara-like confectionery department, and by standing in a queue twice running, again with a feeling of guilt, she got two half-pound packets of a good brand, which encouraged her to look for fish. At the entrance to the fish department, a large notice said *No kippers, dried haddocks, or sausage meat. Please do not ask; a refusal often offends.* Further depressed by this and by the smell of other fish trying to pretend it was fresh, and wondering as she often had before why sausage meat was fish, she wandered, jaded and footsore, to the umbrella department. Here a young lady with purple lips and finger-nails was reading in a grove of highly priced oiled-silk umbrellas. Mrs Morland enquired whether she could get her umbrella re-covered.

'No re-covering done anywhere now,' said the young lady languidly. 'Government won't allow it. Where's the theatre tickets? Couldn't say, I'm shore.'

Mrs Morland enquired again and was directed to the

ticket bureau. It was now twenty minutes to two and she was hungry and exhausted. There was no one at the counter. She asked an assistant at the watches and clocks close by if he knew where one could be found.

'The gentleman goes to his dinner at a quarter to two,' said the watches and clocks.

'But it's only twenty to two,' said Mrs Morland, looking distractedly at the large clock above the counter.

'I dessay he's gone a bit early,' said the watches and clocks. 'He'll be back at a quarter to three.'

'Oh,' said Mrs Morland, nearly crying with fatigue and annoyance. 'Oh, by the way, you haven't a Service wrist-watch, have you? I've been trying everywhere to get one for one of my sons.'

'None for the last year,' said watches and clocks with gloomy satisfaction, 'and not likely to have any. The Government did say we'd be getting some, but we haven't heard any more.'

Mrs Morland went up to the restaurant, an enormous room covering the whole top floor and full to bursting with shoppers, male and female, in uniform and out of uniform, eating and talking as fast and as loudly as they could. Not a vacant place was to be seen. After walking miserably about the room for some time Mrs Morland found one empty place at a table whose she-occupants, engaged, she gathered from their talk, in some kind of secretarial work in a government office, looked at her with undisguised hostility. At last, a waitress came to give the lunchers their bill and remove the dirty plates.

'Oh, could I have a cup of coffee and—' Mrs Morland began.

'Sorry, I'm attending to these ladies,' said the waitress. 'You'll have to wait your turn. There's a war on.'

Well knowing that complaints would be useless, Mrs Morland got up and left the restaurant. As she passed the haberdashery counter, Fate, suddenly relenting, showed her quantities of elastic in every width except the one she needed, and she laid in a store in desperation, feeling a certain pleasure in at last having something to put in her shopping-bag, even if it wasn't what she wanted.

'Oh Lord!' she said as she came out into the street. 'George Knox's book. Well, it will have to be a taxi this time.'

A short drive brought her to Rutland Gate where the Knoxes' depressing family mansion stood, looking with its peeling paint, shrapnel-pocked front and broken boarded-up windows even more depressing than usual. When Mrs Morland had rung several times, the caretaker came to the door and, recognising Mrs Morland as a friend of the family, opened it wide enough to let her in.

'Good afternoon, Mrs Ramsden,' said Mrs Morland. 'Mr Knox wants a book out of the library. Is that all right?'

Mrs Ramsden shut the front door and Mrs Morland came into the hall. The house, which had not been inhabited since the air-raids of the preceding winter except in a mole-like way by Mrs Ramsden who lived in the basement with a varying number of her family, struck a chill to the visitor's heart and her body. In the half-darkness made by the boarded-up windows she could dimly see furniture dust-sheeted and dirty marks on the walls where the pictures had hung. The carpets were rolled up against the walls and there was a general flavour of mushroom beds. In the library the shutters were barred over the shattered windows. Mrs Ramsden turned on the electric light.

'I'd light a fire for you, miss,' said Mrs Ramsden, who was no respecter nor noticer of persons, 'but the Gas aren't giving us any gas, leastways if I turn the fire on here I can't boil my kettle in the kitchen, but I dare say you'll manage.'

Mrs Morland assured her that it would be all right, listened to her story of her daily fight against dirt and damp, not to speak of the ARP Wardens whom she looked upon as her natural enemies, and gave her some tea which she had thoughtfully brought from her store. She then turned to her business of finding the book. The room under the unshaded light was inexpressibly dreary. Soot had fallen down the chimney and tarnish lay on all the bright objects. She drew aside the dust-sheet which covered one of the bookcases and found the book she wanted without much difficulty.

'Goodbye, Mrs Ramsden,' she called down the kitchen stairs.

A clumping noise was heard and Mrs Ramsden's head and shoulders rose majestically from the depths.

'I don't like to write to Mr Knox,' said Mrs Ramsden, whose dislike was founded rather on her splendid immunity to any school education than on any personal grounds, 'so would you tell him a lady come to see about billeting people here if there was any more blitzes, so I said all the beds was occupied. I don't hold with strangers in the house while *I'm* here.'

'Quite right, Mrs Ramsden,' said Mrs Morland, anxious to please one who she felt was far more capable and wiser in ancient wisdom than she could ever be, and at the same time wondering whether in a properly run country she would be hanged for such words.

She then went into the street, where she was lucky enough to see a cruising taxi, so she hailed it and got in, almost too tired to tell it to go to the station. In the little mirror fixed over the opposite seat she caught sight of her own face looking haggard and, she had to confess, rather dirty. Her gloves were covered with thick sooty dirt from the library, reminding her horribly of the sticky substance that Mr Guppy and Mr Weevle touched at Mr Krook's house. She wished, as she mostly did after these visits, that she need never see London again till civilisation had returned.

But blessed be the London Stations where civilisation is not yet quite submerged. On the platform, where the four o'clock was waiting for her in unhurried calm, was a tea trolley, from which not only an inestimable cup of tea could be procured, but packets of biscuits and potato chips, of both which Mrs Morland shamelessly bought as many as she could. Fortified by her tea, she tottered into the train and fell into an exhausted sleep which lasted till the station before High Rising.

When she got back to the house, Stoker was just taking the tea-things into the drawing-room.

'I don't suppose you got the fish,' was her greeting, 'so as I was down in the village I found two lovely kippers. And I knew you wouldn't find a kettle, but Mr Reid at the Stores had some just come in, nice machine-made ones and cheap too, so I got a couple. And Sid Brown's uncle, the one that used to be in Tooting till he was bombed, says he'll do your umbrella, he used to work for one of the big shops there. There isn't no chocolate, nor no elastic, stands to reason, so we'll do without. Same with biscuits and potato chips. Mr Reid says the Government won't let them make any more.'

'Here are two packets of chocolate and a great deal of elastic,' said Mrs Morland coldly. 'And will you ring up Mr Knox and say I got his book. Oh, and here are some biscuits and some potato chips.'

'Well, you *did* have a nice day in town,' said Stoker admiringly.

'Oh, I don't know,' said Mrs Morland, suddenly so

tired and depressed that she could have lain down on the floor and died. 'It was mostly rudeness and nothing to buy.'

'Well, you didn't do so bad,' said Stoker generously. 'And there's a letter from Mr Tony. He'll be an officer before we know where we are.'

Mrs Morland almost snatched the letter from her youngest son which Stoker, who disdained trays, produced from her apron pocket.

'I'll just wash some of the dirt off and then I'm ready for tea,' she said.

A few minutes later, comforted by steaming tea, stayed with the fruit cake that Stoker still mysteriously managed to make, Mrs Morland sat warming her feet before the fire and reading Tony's letter, written from the camp where he was learning to be an artillery officer. Tony appeared to be in good spirits. He did not say that he was wet, cold, hungry, penniless, coughing, overworked, to all of which complaints Mrs Morland was so accustomed that she had almost succeeded in believing that her youngest son exaggerated his miseries; as indeed he did, for parents must be kept on the qui vive. So his mother's spirit rested for a while; and as she reflected on the things that she had succeeded in buying, on the promise of brandy, on the niceness of Mr Siskin and Mr Hopkins, on the reliability of Mrs Ramsden, on Sid Brown's uncle who would re-cover her umbrella, on all the blessings that were once so common and were now to be counted and cherished, she felt that she had indeed had a very nice day in town.

First published in London Calling: A Salute to America, *1942*

VIRAGO MODERN CLASSICS

HIGH RISING

Angela Thirkell

Successful novelist Laura Morland and her boisterous son Tony set off to spend Christmas at her country home in the sleepy surrounds of High Rising. But Laura's wealthy neighbour George Knox has taken on a scheming secretary whose designs on marriage threaten the delicate social fabric of the village. Can clever, practical Laura rescue George from Miss Grey's clutches and, what's more, help his daughter Miss Sibyl Knox to secure her longed-for engagement?

Irresistibly entertaining and witty, *High Rising*, originally published in 1933, was the first of Angela Thirkell's celebrated classic comedies.

'A terrific holiday story'
The Lady

VIRAGO MODERN CLASSICS

WILD STRAWBERRIES

Angela Thirkell

Pretty, impecunious Mary Preston, newly arrived as a guest of her Aunt Agnes at the magnificent wooded estate of Rushwater, falls head over heels for handsome playboy David Leslie. Meanwhile, Agnes and her mother, the eccentric matriarch Lady Emily, have hopes of a different, more suitable match for Mary. At the lavish Rushwater dance party, her future happiness hangs in the balance . . .

Wild Strawberries is a sparkling romantic comedy from Angela Thirkell's much-loved series.

VIRAGO MODERN CLASSICS

POMFRET TOWERS

Angela Thirkell

Pomfret Towers, Barsetshire seat of the earls of Pomfret, was constructed with great pomp and want of concern for comfort in the once-fashionable style of Sir Gilbert Scott's St Pancras station. It makes a grand setting for a house party at which gamine Alice Barton and her brother Guy are guests, mixing with the headstrong Rivers family, the tally-ho Wicklows and, most congenial of all, Giles Foster, nephew and heir of the present Lord Pomfret. But whose hand will Mr Foster seek in marriage, and who will win Alice's tender heart?

Angela Thirkell's 1930s comedy is lively, witty and deliciously diverting.

To buy any of our books and to find out more
about Virago Press and Virago Modern Classics,
our authors and titles, as well as events,
visit our websites

www.virago.co.uk
www.littlebrown.co.uk

and follow us on Twitter

@ViragoBooks

To order any Virago titles p&p-free in the UK,
please contact our mail order supplier on

+ 44 (0)1832 737525

Customers not based in the UK should contact
the same number for appropriate postage
and packing costs.